A MAN NAMED SHONTO

They were already hanging Marshal Holder when Shonto rode into town. It was one hell of a welcome for a loner with a gun but Shonto sensed that things were going to get even worse. He was right. The marshal's body was still swinging from the cottonwood across the street from his own jailhouse when the town became a bloody battleground. At that point, Shonto had just two choices: shoot to kill or join the lawman in hell.

Books by Ryan Bodie
in the Linford Western Library:

WHISKEYVILLE
LOBO
IN THE NAME OF THE GUN
LAST MILE TO NOGALES

RYAN BODIE

A MAN
NAMED
SHONTO

Complete and Unabridged

LINFORD
Leicester

First published in Great Britain in 2010 by
Robert Hale Limited
London

First Linford Edition
published 2011
by arrangement with
Robert Hale Limited
London

British Library CIP Data

Bodie, Ryan.
  A man named Shonto. - -
  (Linford western library)
  1. Western stories.
  2. Large type books.
  I. Title II. Series
  823.9'2–dc22

ISBN 978–1–4448–0680–9

Published by
F. A. Thorpe (Publishing)
Anstey, Leicestershire

Set by Words & Graphics Ltd.
Anstey, Leicestershire
Printed and bound in Great Britain by
T. J. International Ltd., Padstow, Cornwall

This book is printed on acid-free paper

1

Rogue Rope

They were hanging Marshal Holder when Shonto rode into Drum.

The Feather River hellions were behind it. They'd been drinking and brawling for three days straight before the towners wearied of the chaos and pushed the marshal into doing something about it.

Holder had unwisely attempted to arrest the ringleader, Wild Johnny Travis, a young waddy with a lightning fast right hand and the temperament of a rattler. The marshal got the idea of arresting his man after stumbling across him dead drunk in a back alley. Had he managed to get him back to the jailhouse and inside a cell there was a good chance that the towners would have rallied to help their peace officer

1

pacify the rest of the bunch.

It could have worked, but didn't.

The marshal's luck ran out when Wild Johnny's sweetheart from Red Hetty's pleasure palace sighted him dragging her man along Nations Street by his shirt collar. She began screaming so loud it brought a dozen liquored-up hardcases and citizens at the run.

The brawl that followed turned into a full-scale riot when Wild Johnny recovered. There were three men wounded and the barber shop was burning before somebody in that drunken bunch fetched a good length of rope to fit around Steve Holder's neck and they strung him up off the cottonwood directly across the street from his own jailhouse.

With faces daubed by yellow torchlight and brandishing bottles, the wild mob was singing at full volume as the unnoticed horseman appeared around the hotel corner and reined in:

We gone and hanged the marshal
To a sour apple tree,

2

Yes we did,
Yes we did!

Travis and his bunch were leading the chanting as the lifeless body turned slowly in the night wind coming off the Gila, but to their shame there were towners joining in also now.

The shambling ape of violence that lurked in the shadows of every western town had been set loose in Drum that night. Fed on liquor and brought into roaring life by uproar and murder, the beast now shambled unchecked through lamplit streets. The ape was mirrored in every flame-splashed face when the mob assembled before the jailhouse, a fearsome sight for anyone untainted by booze or blood.

But if this grisly spectacle offended the newcomer, he gave no sign as he sat his saddle to draw deeply on a short black cheroot.

Both drunks and onlookers who noted this seeming indifference to what had taken place here, saw a man lean and bronzed by border suns. His shoulders were strong and he dressed in varying shades of brown, his flashy style more like a dude's than an everyday drifter or a man of the land. He carried a sawed-off shotgun rammed into a saddle scabbard and wore a Peacemaker in a swivel holster upon his right hip.

Nobody had seen him in Drum before; he was the kind you would clearly remember.

The mob eventually lost interest in the spectacle of the dead lawman, and began to break up. Excitement and violence had stimulated them, but now the after-effects were beginning to set in. Before the night was out, some would genuinely regret what had happened and a handful might even be ashamed. But feeling sorry wasn't going to help Steve Holder any now.

The bartender at the Panhandle Saloon had played no part in the grisly affair apart from supplying the liquor the mob had required to build up to its full head of steam. It suited him now to appear solemn and regretful as men came in off the street in search of something to take away the bad taste in their mouths.

'Helluva thing,' he lamented. 'Here we were without a lawman for three months on account nobody had the guts to take on the lousy job. Then, soon as we get one, we hang the poor bastard. Ain't that a caution?'

Nobody answered.

The barkeep's gloomy eye fell upon the stranger in the flash brown jacket.

'You see what happened out there, friend?' he asked.

Shonto shouldered a drinker aside to breast the long bar. His lips barely moved as he studied the bottles. 'Yeah.'

'What did you think of it?'

'Seen one lynching, you've seen them all.'

The bartender rolled his eyes. He was surrounded by savages without normal human feelings. He felt so badly about all the violence in the world that when he got home later that night he might have to beat up his wife in order to feel a little better.

★ ★ ★

Red Hetty's visits to the Drum Bank every Monday, Wednesday and Friday morning were a regular routine unaffected by heat, rain, riot, acts of God or even the occasional death upon the streets.

Always handsomely decked out in whatever happened to be the latest fashion, the madam of Drum's thriving Nations Street bordello would set out with her bulging black purse slung over one shoulder, a veil over her face to show she was a lady and a two-shot Smith & Wesson concealed upon her generously proportioned person — just in case.

Hetty could have an escort any time she wanted, for she employed two genuine hard men back at the house just to keep things under control. But to have done so might suggest she lacked the confidence and ability to look out for herself — both qualities any red-blooded madam must possess in order to be taken seriously in a place like Drum.

Respect was what it was all about, and Hetty had it.

The last time someone had tried to relieve the madam of the takings, her single shot fired from the hip cured the would-be thief of two vices. He never attempted to rob another woman on her way to the bank and permanently lost all interest in visiting either Hetty's or any other pleasure house along the river.

'Sometimes I feel I'm the toughest man in town,' she would often boast with a drink or two under her garter belt. And, after a couple more, would genuinely believe it.

Today, Hetty made one slight change to her regular route by crossing Nations Street before reaching the jailhouse. Someone had cut the body down overnight but the rope still dangled from the lowest branch, sinister and motionless in the still air.

Hetty was no great admirer of the opposite sex, and even though she'd had no reason to feel kindly towards the late Marshal Holder, she still felt badly about what had occurred. She liked things free and easy, but felt they were getting far too much that way in Drum these days.

She thought it was one thing for men to raise hell and have a fine old time drinking and chasing pretty girls. But it was something else when they went loco and got to do just about whatever they liked while everybody else just sat back and watched.

In such a place, she reflected, nobody was really safe — not even a long-legged, Smith & Wesson packing businesswoman.

'Mornin', ma'am,' the teller welcomed on her arrival. He was a solemn, bespectacled younger man who never addressed her by name for fear someone might suspect undue familiarity. He was a respectable young man who only visited Hetty's twice a month — late at night. 'I say, did you hear about the — '

'No, and I don't want to,' Hetty cut him off. She cast a critical look around at the other customers, every one of them male.

She raised her voice: 'I must say I'm surprised to see all you fine gentlemen here this morning, looking so hale and hearty. When I looked from my window last night and saw the marshal in peril I didn't sight a single one of you. I thought you must have all been out of town.'

The only man not to appear embarrassed came forward and gave a gracious bow.

'My dear Miss Hetty. And how are you this fine morning? Or is there any need for me to ask that when I can see by the colour in your cheek and the sparkle in your eyes that you are, as always, in the pink. Or should that be red? Heh, heh.'

Humphrey Collier was mayor of Drum, a large and florid man who could laugh his head off without a hint of real humour ever reaching his eyes. As the town's banker and most successful businessman, Collier had a finger in many a pie around town and owned a solid forty percent interest in Hetty's establishment. He was a frequent visitor to the place on Nations Street, but only to drink and enjoy the convivial atmosphere. He could have women without paying. He was one of the few men in town Hetty was forced to respect, but that didn't make her like him.

'Why, you seem remarkably jolly for a mayor who's just had his marshal lynched by a drunken mob, Humphrey,' she said, moving to leave.

Collier was quick to get the door. His manners were impeccable, but only when in the mood.

'A disgraceful business, my dear,' he muttered as they stood on the porch. His gesture embraced Nations Street, a broad avenue of yellow dust fronted by adobes, false-fronts and one or two more impressive structures such as his Sunrise Hotel half a block along. 'What's going to become of us if this sort of thing is allowed to continue, I ask you?'

Hetty turned to see two burly men mounting the porch. They nodded gravely to her then took up positions behind Collier and stood with hands behind their backs. The banker's bodyguards were seldom far from his side.

'Nothing will ever change,' Hetty sighed. 'It took us months to find someone willing to pin on a star, and Steve Holder was a tolerably competent man. You can wager nobody will want the job now after what happened to him.'

'That's a pessimistic view I don't share, Hetty. I believe our town has a bright future — '

'Save it for election time, Humphrey,' she sighed, going down the steps. She nodded to the bodyguards. 'See you

11

around, boys. Looks like you'll have to start earning your money again now there's no law on the streets, huh?'

Mash and Poulter doffed plug hats and nodded in unison. They were unfailingly polite to Red Hetty whom they rightly regarded as a major player in the town. Yet they weren't too concerned that the sheriff's death might throw added responsibility their way. The mayor was so strong in Drum that not even the Feather River boys dared bother him.

It was that wild bunch that occupied Hetty's thoughts as she made her way across the street then mounted the walk. They were regular customers and she even liked some of them . . . Flint and Holly, for instance.

But they were all getting way out of hand. In the aftermath of last night it was plain things couldn't continue this way much longer.

She was turning into the hotel when she met the stranger coming out. He stepped aside and touched his hat brim.

Hetty gave him a cursory glance, then halted to stare back at him.

The man paused to meet her gaze and appeared faintly amused. He was a stranger, and as strangers had been involved in last night's bloody affair, her stare turned suspicious.

'And who might you be?'

'Name's Shonto.'

'Is that a first name or last name.'

'Both.'

'You mean you only have the one?'

'Ain't one enough?'

She couldn't tell if he was trying to make a fool of her. She could not read him, and that bothered a woman who rightly regarded herself as an authority on the entire male species.

'So, tell me . . . Shonto, were you involved in that lynching affair?'

'Sorry, just missed it, Hetty.'

She frowned. 'How did you know my name?'

He spread hands that were slender and supple. 'Why, I saw you strolling by earlier and seeing as though you were the

13

first thing in this yellow town I liked the look of, I had to ask who you were.'

She felt flattered, yet somehow challenged as well.

'Yellow town? That is a pretty quick conclusion to jump to from someone who's barely had time to hang his hat up, isn't it?'

'I only call them as I see them . . . Hetty.'

'So, you think Drum is cowardly?'

'Not think. Know.'

'Then I guess you won't be staying?' she challenged huffily.

'Didn't say that, Hetty.' He looked her up and down. 'This might be a yellow town, but I never said it wasn't interesting.'

She lifted her chin as his steady gaze rested on her breasts. 'I don't think I like you, Mr Shonto.'

His smile softened the taut hardness of his features.

'Well, ma'am, all I can say is, if you ever get to starting an I-Hate-Shonto-Club you'll never be short of members.'

He touched hat brim and turned away. 'Adios for now, Miss Red Hetty.'

'What a smart ass!' Hetty muttered tartly as she walked off. Yet that wasn't how she was thinking an hour later while taking coffee with several of her drowsy, half-dressed working girls in her plush velvet upstairs parlour on Nations Street. Now she appeared wistful as she gazed from the window at a slow-passing buggy below. 'You know, babies, I do believe I struck something unusual earlier . . . something I do believe I must have almost forgotten about. Yes . . . a vanishing breed you might say . . . '

The girls stared. A soft or sentimental Hetty was a rarity here.

Dark-eyed Libby yawned; it had been a busy night on River Street following the lynching.

'A vanishing breed of what, Hetty?' she asked drowsily.

'Why, the rarest of the very rare, particularly here.' Her eyes brightened. 'I do believe I encountered a real man.'

15

'Ain't no such critter,' young and cynical Gina declared.

'And if there is, then he's never been to Drum,' Carmelita put in.

'Oh . . . maybe you could be right.' Hetty sighed, then snapped back into business mode in an instant. 'Well, my sugars, let's get busy and straighten things up before they start pourin' in on us.'

'This early?' Libby looked dismayed. 'But they never start before noon.'

'Today they will,' Red Hetty said briskly, getting to her feet. 'Today they'll be squirmin' with guilt, and they'll roll in here tryin' to get rid of it. And you know somethin', my honeys . . .'

'Yeah, we know,' Gina sighed. 'We'll get rid of the guilt for them. And why so, girls?' She paused to allow the others to join in. 'Because whatever the customer wants the customer gets!' they chorused.

Their words were laced with irony, but Red Hetty didn't object. She wasn't concerned with morality, or lack of it, only in making herself rich. She only hoped that despite the way things were heading here lately she might manage to stay alive and keep her place from being burned to the ground before she actually did become rich.

Retiring wealthy was her single remaining ambition. She had long ago discarded her original girlish dream of winding up wealthy with a real man at her side. If any woman had dreams of winning a real man, her first step would have to be — leave Drum.

* * *

'You dealt that ace out of your sleeve,' Shonto said.

He didn't speak loudly yet his voice carried around the bar room of the Panhandle Saloon. Conversations petered out and the chink of glassware and dice faded into silence. Drinkers and percentage girls turned to stare across at the poker layout where every player was now looking at Shacklock, the man accused.

Shacklock reacted swiftly. No Feather River rider could take that sort of insult in Drum. Kicking his chair back with a crash he dropped right hand to gunbutt and faced his accuser.

'Nobody calls me a cheat! Get on your feet and back it up, dude!'

This was the cue for every player to vacate his chair. Everybody knew Shacklock as a fiery customer, and from what they'd seen of this new man in town he didn't match up.

Veterans of past poker games which had erupted into violence caught the whiff of gunsmoke in the air.

Shonto appeared to smile as he studied the cards in his hand. His hat was pushed to the back of his head and his lean body appeared totally relaxed.

'Sit down before you wet your pants, sonny,' he drawled.

Shacklock turned livid. As a pard of Wild Johnny Travis and a key member of the Feather River bunch, he had an image to maintain.

And yet he half-hesitated, and studying him more closely now, Shonto realized why. For behind the tough façade he saw that Shacklock was a phoney; he could pick the breed a block away.

'You don't want to shoot me just because you're such a lousy card cheat, sonny,' he murmured, leaning back in his chair.

'I ain't no cheat!' Shacklock's voice was growing louder.

'Sure you are. Dragging that ace out of your shirt was as clumsy as I've seen. Others saw it too, but I guess they're too scared to say so. So, it looks like it's left to me to straighten you out. But let's get rid of that gun first, then fish out the rest of the cards you've got up your sleeve and pay us all back what you owe. Then we'll have a drink together and forget all about it.'

The last vestige of colour drained from the waddy's face. The knuckles of the hand wrapped around six-gun handle turned white.

'Why, you goddamn dude!' he snarled. 'I can outgun your kind blindfold — right where you're settin'!'

Shonto shrugged and onlookers held their breath at his seeming unawareness of the danger he was in.

'Of course you can't do that, boy, you only think you can. Now, about the cheating — '

He got no further as Shacklock grabbed for gun handle. In one casual motion, Shonto lifted his right foot beneath the table then kicked upwards hard. The leading edge caught Shack-lock square in the guts slamming him backwards with cards, bottles, money and glasses flying in confusion.

Shacklock was doubled over and clutching at himself with his jaws wide open but with no sound coming out, his face white as death. Calmly, Shonto seized his right wrist then fingered two high cards from the man's shirtsleeve. He released his grip and Shacklock slumped to the floor, sucking in a little air at last. Shonto bent and collected five dollars from the money scattered on the floor, then straightened.

'Well, you could call it interesting, I guess,' he said to the gaping crowd. 'But if I had my way I'd have a quiet game any day.'

He sauntered out and staff and hangers-on hastened to help Shacklock into a chair. As someone fetched water and colour returned to the man's sallow cheeks, everybody began talking at once.

Yet every man sensed the incident wouldn't end there. The reason? Shacklock had friends here. Dangerous friends.

2

Red Hetty's House

'I'll serve the man, Polly,' insisted Greasy Abe, the overweight proprietor of the Drum Hash House. 'You just keep an eye on these here taters and see they don't burn none.'

Polly Gearin was puzzled. Abe rarely waited on tables for the good reason that he tended to scare off customers. No change-daily man, Greasy Abe usually sported a three-day growth of whiskers and wore a Mexican sombrero with bobbing eagle feathers thrust through the band. Everyone but Abe himself agreed he was far better placed in the kitchen than out front when the paying customers were taking breakfast.

'But why, Abe?' Polly said.

'Don't start questionin' how I run my own place, girl,' he warned. 'I reckon I can serve my own customers in my own goddamn time when I want, can't I?'

'I suppose.' Polly was just eighteen and prettier than a heart flush. As delicate as a flower and poor as a church mouse, most everybody in Drum saw it as their duty to protect pretty Polly from some of the harsher realities of life. In this adobe town, sprawled around a sluggish hook in the Gila, reality could be harsh as the hobs of hell. She pouted prettily. 'But if you don't think I'm up to waiting on tables, you really should let me go.'

Abe rolled his eyeballs. He was just one of her many admirers and protectors. Sweet, virginal girls were so scarce in Drum that most citizens tended to be overprotective to the mere handful the town did have.

'Polly,' he said in what was intended to be a whisper, 'I ain't sayin' you ain't up to the job. I just don't want to see you waitin' on desperadoes like that one.'

Greasy Abe's whisper boomed into a tin soup kettle and was accidentally magnified and projected out into the room occupied by a Scandinavian wheat farmer and his wife, a drunk making a mess of a bowl of soup, two cowhands, a miner, and Shonto.

Shonto reckoned there was no prize for guessing who Greasy Abe was referring to.

'Where's my coffee?' he called.

'See, what'd I tell you,' Abe hissed at Polly. 'No manners and no class neither.'

'But, Abe, nobody who comes here has any class.'

That hit Greasy Abe where it hurt. In his mind the Drum Hash House was the best eating place in town. He was offended to think anybody might feel differently.

'Polly, are you goin' to give me that pot or — '

'No, Abe, I'm sorry but I'm not. If I'm to work here I shouldn't have to be protected against anybody.' She paused to peer out into the diner. 'In any case, he doesn't look so bad to me.'

'That's because you are just a babe in the woods. Did you see what he done to Shacklock? He's put that man in bed for a week, so the doc tells me. He's mean-mouthed, quick-tempered and sports a funny kinda trick pistol. So how can you say he don't look bad?'

But Polly simply flashed a reassuring smile and, pot and coffee mug from the kitchen in hand, threaded her way through the tables to the front window table where cigar smoke hazed the glass.

'I'm sorry for the delay, Mr Shonto,' she dimpled. 'We couldn't get the coffee to boil.'

Shonto watched her pour. Hatless and clean-shaven today, he appeared relaxed and expressionless. Thick dark hair flowed back from his broad brow in waves and Polly noted how he seemed to exude a purely masculine power, yet held it in check.

'Cream and sugar?' she asked.

'Do I look like cream and sugar?'

She blushed again and gave a hesitant smile. She found his very maleness disconcerting.

'Are you enjoying your visit to our town, Mr Shonto?'

'I'll bet you say that to all your drop-ins.'

She sobered. She had a habit of taking people seriously even when they might be sarcastic, ironic or just plain pulling her leg. 'I'm sure you're not just any no-account drop-in, Mr Shonto. You appear to be quite a nice gentleman to me.'

His eyebrows lifted. 'Nice? Well, I reckon I'm as nice as they come, honey, but I got to admit it's been quite a time since anybody told me so.'

'Polly.'

'Huh?'

'That's my name. Polly Gearin.'

Shonto slowly lowered his mug, disarmed. He scanned her face and his flinty look eased some. 'Well, that's a swell name, Polly Gearin. You can call me Shonto, forget the mister.'

She was serious again. 'Has anybody warned you of the danger you could be in after what happened at the saloon?'

'Why don't you tell me about it?'

Polly leaned closer confidentially.

'You probably don't know it, but Mr Shacklock comes from Feather River, and the fellers from down there are all kind of wild. I fear that when Mr Shacklock's friends hear what has happened they will arrive here with mischief on their minds. They seem to believe they can do just whatever they want in Drum, and they simply hate it if anybody dares stand up to them.'

'Well, thanks for your warning, Polly,' Shonto said gravely, as though hearing this advice for the first time. He drained his coffee, pressed a coin into the girl's hand and gave a small bow as he rose. 'I only plan staying a day or so, but if I meet those Feather River jokers I'll keep what you said in mind. Much obliged.'

Only an innocent could fail to detect

the irony in his voice, but an innocent Polly Gearin surely was. She retreated to the kitchen and shot Greasy Abe a look of heavy reproof.

'Well, Abe, you were completely wrong about Mr Shonto. He's a real gentleman.'

The man's eyeballs rolled. For he'd been present at the Panhandle when that Shonto floored Shacklock and likely put a permanent crimp in his love life. He'd seen all kinds come and go in Drum but already had Shonto tabbed as maybe seriously dangerous. This suggested that sweet Polly Gearin had a long way to go before she might be considered safe in the real world of men.

'Will you go clean up after Drunky John, honey?' he asked gently. 'He's spilled his soup over again.'

Polly hurried off to handle the chore. As she swabbed the table she glanced out into the street to see Shonto now leaning idly against an upright on the Panhandle porch and admiring a young

Mexican girl passing by.

She sighed.

He still looked like a gentleman to her. But as Greasy Abe might remark, would she really know one if she saw one?

*   *   *

The poorer women of Drum took their washing to the Gila to scrub it clean against the rocks in running water that had risen in the mountains of western New Mexico then came flowing across Arizona to the Colorado River at Yuma and down the Gila Valley to ripple and chuckle its way over the shining river stones of Drum on its long journey south.

They were Mexican women mostly, for the white ladies had boilers for their wash, or else hired women like these to do it for them. They didn't mind the work and mostly found it enjoyable to be out of doors trading gossip and getting to see a little of what was going on in their limited world.

They were hard at it when one happened to glance up and sight the lean figure standing on the high bank gazing down at them. The woman nudged her companion, and pretty soon everyone was sneaking a look at the stranger, now puffing a short black cigar.

'That is him,' one murmured, 'the one who beat up on Shacklock.'

'You sound envious, Maria,' another teased. 'Do you wish perhaps he had attacked you. He seems *mucho hombre*.'

The first woman spat. 'He is as all are who come to Drum. No good for anything but fighting, drinking and killing.'

'Perhaps this one may see more of such things than he might wish should he still be here when Shacklock and his *amigos* come to town,' a third woman speculated. 'Now that we have no sheriff, who is to keep these wild ones in check?'

Shonto could hear the voices above

the murmur of the river, but not what was being said.

His face was in hat shadow as he turned away to tread the gravelled pathway flanking the river. He strolled with thumbs hooked in shell belt and shirt unbuttoned to the sun. His pace neither fast nor slow, he did a complete circuit of the town which finally brought him back to Nations Street near the livery where his horse was stalled.

The liveryman was grooming the animal when Shonto appeared in the doorway. He was Mexican-American, a familiar breed here in a town which was no longer one thing or the other, neither the sleepy adobe hideaway of the past nor the modern American town it one day might become.

Shonto was greeted with a toothy smile.

'He is a fine horse, *señor.*'

'He's crowbait.'

'*Señor?*'

'He's not fast, he can't last and he's

got a lousy disposition. I call him Wolf because the only thing he does really well is bite.'

The liveryman massaged his arm. He had already been bitten. He resumed his chore while keeping one wary eye on the horse's head.

'A very hot day, *señor*.'

'I've seen hotter.'

'Of course, of course. Do you like our town?'

Shonto rested a thigh on the edge of a scarred work bench. He took out a cheroot, cracked a match on his thumbnail and inhaled a lungful of good smoke before replying.

'I've seen better.'

'It was a very good town once . . . before . . . '

The man's voice trailed away and he focused on his grooming.

'Before we came, you mean?' Shonto prompted. 'Gringos?'

'No, I was not going to say that, *señor*.'

'Sure you were.'

Shonto got up and went to the doorway, leaning a shoulder against the jamb.

'Anyway, you're right,' he commented after a silence. 'This was all better before the Americans came west. You had a handful of folks here who lived like kings while the rest of you starved and liked it. Life was uncomplicated. But when we came along and told you everybody was equal, you suckers swallowed it. As a consequence the dons have now been replaced by gringo businessmen and you still go hungry with the seat out of your pants. Tell me I'm wrong.'

'You seem bitter, Señor Shonto.'

'Realistic, mebbe.' Shonto looked up at the shimmering blue arch of the sky. 'Too hot for riding. I'll stop by later.'

'Later may be too late, *señor*,' the man was moved to warn.

Shonto knew what he meant, but let it ride. He wasn't running for any reason. Not here. Not any place.

The noon sun was like a weight

across his shoulders as he headed off along River Street. On a corner ahead stood the two-storeyed frame house that had been Drum's leading hotel before Mayor Collier built the Sunrise. The building was freshly painted with bright, striped canvas curtains shading the windows. It was surrounded by a high fence and a lamp with a cherry-red globe hung from a bracket in the entrance.

The doors stood open in silent invitation and he strolled in. The ornate lobby was cool and gloomy with heavy curtains drawn tightly against the glare. Blue-shaded lamps glowed from the bar area and girls in skimpy working costumes stirred lazily upon the velvet couches as he crossed to the bar.

'Tequila and salsa,' he said to the pale blonde, and leaned an elbow on the bar. 'And just in case you were about to ask, honey — no, I'm not quitting town.'

She fixed his drink. She was young, but her way of life made her feel like she was chalking up three years for every one she spent at Red Hetty's. She eyed him speculatively as he tossed change on to the bar. 'You're Shonto, aren't you?'

He nodded, tasted the peppery red salsa in the shot glass and then downed his drink. He nodded approvingly.

A door opened and Red Hetty appeared with fiery red hair piled high and a modest gown buttoned snugly at wrists and throat. Her gesture dispatched the others to the lobby. She crossed to Shonto, frowning.

'What brings you here?' she wanted to know.

'Why, what have you got?'

She faced him squarely without smiling. 'I'm being serious.'

'So am I.' He leaned back. 'Well, at least let's say I'm as serious as any man would be who is asked what he's doing here.'

Hetty slid onto a stool, the slit in her gown revealing a length of silken leg.

'If I may say so, you don't look at all

like a customer to me.'

Wordlessly, Shonto held up his glass.

She frowned. 'I'm not talking about the booze and you know it,' she said tersely. 'Experience has taught me that men of your, well . . . style, don't need to visit places that offer special services, like mine.' She paused a moment, then added, 'I might as well be frank, Mr Shonto. I'd rather you didn't visit my establishment.'

'Are you telling me to go?'

'No. It's a free country. But I certainly would like you to leave.'

'Sooo . . . this is all about the ruckus I had, eh, Miss Hetty? Is that it? Hell, I'd have figured a woman of the world like yourself would have seen it all and got so that a bit of a rough-house didn't worry you any longer.'

'You are aware, of course, that Johnny Travis and those other Feather River hellions will be coming in after you?'

Shonto turned the glass slowly in his fingers. He raised it to his lips and sipped sparingly, the woman watching his every movement.

'Just about everyone I've met has been happy to warn me I could get killed here,' he remarked drily. 'Even the dogs are yapping it.' He turned on his stool to face the doors where a beam of hot yellow sunlight showed. 'But I came quite a ways to get here and I'm just getting settled. I don't aim to cut and run just because someone mightn't like the way I handled him.' He shrugged. 'So, I'm making myself at home for now, and folks are always saying home is the best place a man can be.'

'How can you treat the possibility of getting maimed or killed as some kind of joke?'

But Shonto did not reply. Suddenly bored with the conversation, his gaze turned remote, and after several attempts to engage him again had failed, Hetty left him alone.

One by one, the girls returned but none approached the solitary figure at the bar. Nobody was shy in this place, but like Hetty herself all now sensed it wasn't women that had brought this visitor here today.

'And . . . more's the pity,' Gina lamented. 'I mean, how come the first genuinely interesting-looking feller to walk into this dump in months acts like he's got more important things on his mind than a quick stroll upstairs? What's the world coming to, I ask you!'

'Perhaps he is thinking of dying?' speculated dramatic Carmelita, a Mexican beauty with a natural affinity for sad endings.

'Killing, more likely,' Gina speculated, resting bare arms on the back of a sofa while studying their visitor with torpid interest. 'Uh-huh, he looks to me like somebody who would kill without his conscience raising an eyebrow.' She licked her lips. 'Those hands . . . so lean yet strong . . . mmm . . . '

Her voice faded and one of those torpid silences that can come to any plush bordello on a sultry afternoon engulfed the room. It was not to be disturbed until the distant drum of hoofbeats sounded from the direction of the river a half-hour on.

Shonto raised one eyebrow and it seemed to his pretty watchers that a flicker of either annoyance or regret crossed his features. Then the look was gone and he rose lazily to move to the centre of the room where he paused as if to admire the plush surrounds.

'Only hope your boss lady appreci-ates what I'm doing for her, ladies,' he murmured, putting on his hat.

'Just what are you doing, Mr Shonto?' Gina drawled.

'Why, for one thing, I'll be going off so's not to mess up her nice bordello should someone raise the dust.' He slapped his pivot gun and although his expression was sober, there was a mocking note in his tone as he added, 'But I'll be back . . . bank on that.'

He was gone. The girls traded looks and soon heard the hoofbeats approaching along Nations Street, mingled with the shouting.

All guessed who it was and some feared for the gunfighter and dreaded the outcome. Yet not even Red Hetty was able to stop them from donning their prettiest dresses and skipping down to Nations Street to go watch the 'fun'.

3

Young Men Die Fast

Mostly when the Feather River boys came to town, Jack Henry rode lead.

A barrel-chested husky with sweeping moustaches, Henry was never sighted without twin six-shooters. In the absence of Wild Johnny Travis today, Henry rated as top gun in the hardcase bunch that made their home in the remote ghost town of Feather River. Aggressive and edgy by nature, Henry appeared double-mean today as he let his horse trot on by the livery stables then onwards past the heavy shade trees out front of the Sunrise Hotel on his way to the Panhandle.

He was trailed by Holly and Flint, the so-called 'six-gun twins' of the outfit, a pair of gunners who'd made Arizona their home after evading the

41

hangman's noose in their native Texas. Killers all.

Not a shred of conscience or compassion amongst the whole bunch — or at least that was how the town saw them.

Riding proud and straight as they saw the interest they were arousing, the Texans cut their eyes this way and that searching for the man they'd come to kill.

Felix Bax brought up the rear. Of a different breed from the others in most every way, he was a tall and slender Easterner with a Virginia culture behind him. A gunman with knobs of pride set one on top of each other like spinal vertebrae, he'd recently risen to become the front man of the bunch whenever trouble threatened. Travis's bosom pard, Bax, impressed the womenfolks all over — providing they were not the squeamish kind. Cosying up to good-looking Felix could prove an unnerving experience unless a girl was able to put the men he'd slain from her mind.

An air of assurance surrounded the horsemen as they returned the stares of the citizens now gathering to watch them go by along Nations Street.

Only recently Drum Council had set up yet another marshal at the jailhouse whose principal task was to curb Wild Johnny and his kind. The marshal now slept with the angels and these were the men who'd put him there. Yet the bunch didn't regard themselves as butchers or badmen, but rather as the swashbuckling sons of the frontier, too fast to catch and too young to die.

They'd run hog-wild along the Gila for some years now, and part of their code was never to permit any challenge or injury go unanswered.

Bax had secretly visited their pard Shacklock at Doc Stedman's overnight, and came away knowing their saddle pard would never be the same man again thanks to this man, Shonto.

The way the bunch figured, if they were to let anything like this go unanswered this lousy town might get to thinking they were losing their punch.

The hell they were!

'So . . . where is this dirty back-shooter anyway?' Henry shouted as they reined in outside the jailhouse. 'Where is this white-fingered nancy who busted up our pard?'

The voice sent a thrill of expectation humming along the dusty street. Drum was the kind of town that loved action, the bloodier the better.

Felix Bax slowly circled the others astride his magnificent white horse, features handsome and taut.

'Shonto!'

His shout echoed along the false-fronted street, and necks craned as people peered left and right for first sign of the only man in town who'd never seen the bunch before nor knew what they were capable of.

'You sure this sonofa ain't up and hightailed?' Bax called to one of the mayor's bodyguards.

'You can bet he's gone,' growled

Poulter. 'But we better make sure.'

The gang tied up at the hotel hitchrail and trooped inside unchallenged to climb the stairs. They gained the first floor balcony and startled the councillors who'd gathered there to watch, imagining they would be safe at that level. No sign of any gunpacker here.

'Shonto!'

Bax's shout boomed down the from the balcony, and necks craned. There was no response.

'It's plain he's hightailed,' muttered Mash, one of the mayor's bodyguards.

'Sure he has,' whispered his partner, Poulter, squinting nervously down the strip of dusty street. 'Wouldn't you?'

'Five bucks he'll show,' challenged the mayor, who seemed to know something others might not.

Someone covered his wager while others leaned over the railing to scan the street again.

'Still nothing — ' the man named Holly began, but broke off at a sudden shout.

'There he is!'

Nobody knew if one man spoke loudly or many spoke together softly. Yet suddenly Shonto was in clear view as he came around the River Street corner with the unhurried stride of a man on his way to work.

In the crook of his right arm he carried a sawn-off shotgun while sunlight glinted from the metal swivel holster holding the Peacemaker snugged on his right hip. With a cheroot jutting from his teeth he walked the dead centre of main street making directly towards the gunmen when they clattered back downstairs to reach the street.

The four first slowed then halted uncertainly as they met the newcomer's bleak stare, which might have intimidated lesser men.

But they were not lesser men; they were the Feather River Boys and fanned out, ready to prove it.

Shonto came on and Bax called upon him to halt. He maintained the same stride, neither fast nor slow. Even the warning sight of Jack Henry unbuckling the clip which held his .45 snug in its cutaway holster appeared to have no effect on the new man in town.

He drew within fifty feet before he halted. 'Heard you men are looking for me?'

Hands slid closer to gunbutts. The silence was deep and ominous.

'Better get shook of that sawed-off afore we talk, mister,' Henry warned. 'It kinda makes us nervous.'

'Understandable, that,' came the response. 'It could also make you dead!'

'Drop it!' Bax yelled in sudden impatience, fingers firming around the walnut handle of his Colt .44. 'You done a good man wrong and we guns are come here to deal with you. So shuck the shooter and take what's comin' or you'll be dead quicker than a man can spit — that's fair warnin!'

Nothing happened. Shonto stood statue-still and without expression. The gunmen stirred restlessly, then Bax suddenly cursed.

'On the count of three!' he barked at Holly, and slipped into a gunfighter's crouch with right hand hovering over gunbutt.

Holly began counting. Shonto didn't wait for him to reach three and was sliding the hammer of the shotgun back with a loud click as the gunman rasped, 'Two!'

'Don't try it!' was his final warning before Bax's right arm blurred. Shonto leaned back on his heels and squeezed trigger.

The awful roar of the piece rocked the street and Bax was lifted off his feet by the blast that took him full in the chest and flung him backwards, dead before he struck ground.

Without pause Shonto swung smoothly upon Jack Henry and smashed his gun arm with the second charge. Then the sawn-off was cast aside and he palmed the handle of his swivel gun as Holly went into his draw. But the shock of Bax's swift death had half-frozen that gunman, who too late realized his fingers would not respond to his will.

Shonto came forwards and slammed the barrel of his Colt against the man's skull to belt him clear off his feet — and it was all over, as Flint raised his hands in submission.

An onlooker with a calm nerve and reliable timepiece later claimed the whole incident had occupied less than ten seconds from start to finish.

★ ★ ★

Mayor Collier studied the glass of red wine in his hand and spoke the way he always did when the audience was attentive and the dramatist in him rose to the surface.

'Death, what is it?' he asked rhetorically, solemn as a hanging judge. 'A cessation of the senses, a freeing from all earthly desires, a one-way ticket to either eternal joy or the great darkness!'

He paused for effect. Carmelita sniffed loudly and even tough Gina appeared a little misty-eyed. The mayor could capture a mood when in the right frame of mind, and it was possible for even flint-hearted young hookers who would sell their own mothers for a buck to grow sentimental over the demise of a recently departed young man who'd often availed himself of their specialized services in the past.

He nodded solemnly and continued. 'Yet tonight it is safe to assume that Bax is either happier in death than he ever was on earth — or else is burning in greater torment than our imaginations could ever conceive.'

'Never seen shootin' like it,' muttered a bystander, running a finger nervously round his shirt collar.

The good mayor was well under the weather by this stage but his ever-present bodyguards remained sober and alert. It was a fact of life here that so many citizens hated their mayor for so many legitimate reasons that his round-the-clock guard was virtually a necessity.

'It was terrible,' sniffed Gina. 'I

wouldn't have believed a man could die so fast.'

'Only reason Shonto's still walking around in one piece and those two ain't,' put in a mourner who kept ogling the girls, 'is that he must be the fastest sonova we've ever seen. Anyways, it was only fair, the way it all turned out. Them boys came in a bunch to murder the *hombre* and he got in first. And who knows? If they'd have got Shonto they might've turned on us.'

'Some loss that woulda been,' someone said from the back. But nobody responded because the mayor had the floor again.

'Our fair town is becoming one vast graveyard,' he intoned solemnly. 'A massed bier for the young and a final resting place for the slow and the unlucky.'

He raised his glass which someone had thoughtfully refilled. 'To a young man who shall live in our memories forever as ever young ... never to dandle grandchildren on his knee ...

51

poor Felix Baxter. Long may his memory survive!'

The mayor had Bax's name wrong but nobody commented. They knew better. They also knew Humphrey Collier had no more compassion in him than a gila monster. A man didn't rise from poverty to riches and power through being soft. Those who knew the mayor best suspected that the real reason he was letting himself go tonight was from relief that the Feather River gang had just lost their next-to-top gun who'd rated only behind Wild Johnny himself.

It was possible now, with Bax dead, Travis absent and Henry laid up, the mayor might get to assume control again. So it was easy to understand why he felt moved to eloquence.

'To a man who shall be ever enshrined in loving memory as young and gracious . . . never to feel the ache of age in his bones . . . never to dandle a grandchild on his knee . . . '

The voice droned on and the mob

who'd gathered did not interrupt the repetition. For most realized that over recent times the wild bunch from down river had been growing dominant to a point where they were posing a real threat to their town and way of life. Now, with only Wild Johnny still free and unscathed some place, the mayor felt he could move to issue a warning in his own well-oiled way.

'To Wild Johnny!' he boomed, hoisting his glass again. 'May he have the wisdom to learn from this lesson and not visit us again lest he too might join his friends amongst the dead!'

'Fat chance of him listenin' to that,' Red Hetty commented. She was one of the few who hadn't seen the gunfight, and was glad of it. She drew pleasure from seeing men having themselves a good time, not go down coughing blood on a sun-stricken street. 'But Johnny will show up sooner or later, and then you can bet the farm there'll be more shooting if he finds Shonto still here.'

'Speakin' of Shonto,' a portly citizen in a black top hat slurred, 'what happened to him afterwards? Where'd he disappear to?'

Nobody seemed to know.

4

Plant them Deep

The electric murmurings of the approaching thunderstorm stirred the flimsy curtains of the room where the girl slept. Hers was one of the best rooms to be found in Miss Henson's Rooming House yet was still little more than four plain walls enclosing a single bed, narrow bureau and wash stand.

The orphan girl from the arid reaches of Arizona had known it worse than this. Much worse.

Thunder muttered closer and the fields of wild grasses stretching beyond the town limits stirred and whispered before the strengthening wind. A dog whimpered in its sleep as yet another sound, strange and unfamiliar, drifted through the curtained window to disturb Polly's innocent dreams.

What was it?

She sat up on the edge of her narrow bed, a thin figure in a shapeless, all-enveloping gown, blue eyes fixed upon the window. She waited until the sound was repeated but was still unable to guess what it was other than that it could be a human voice.

The scrubbed bare floor was cold beneath her feet as she rose and crossed to the window. The first thing she sighted outside was that awesome, rolling surge of thunderheads climbing up the sky beyond the livery stables. Half the moonlit sky was already engulfed by storm clouds rushing in from the south, purple and black with a wicked greenish aura at the base and a jittery jig of lightning dancing in its depths.

The wind in her face was chill as she stared down, but the storm was instantly forgotten when she sighted the figure sprawled before the stables. At first she thought it was moonlight distorting some object, but then the huddled mass moved slightly and she realized with a sense of shock that it was a man, and not just any man but the one who'd filled Nations Street with the roar of his gun and the stench of death earlier.

Shonto!

She reached up for the window sash, intending to close it before drawing down the blind. For young and innocent though she was she had learned much about drunken men since coming to Drum, and the sprawled figure below — hatless, and dusted in alkali — appeared the classic picture of a victim of demon rum.

A slamming bolt of chain lightning caused her to start and close her eyes. When she opened them again the first raindrops were beginning to fall. She focused her gaze upon the figure below again as he raised a hand to the back of his head and his fingertips came away the colour of blood.

Rain was falling in earnest by the time the girl emerged from the rooming house a short time later. Shonto had somehow made it up to one knee by then. She knelt at his side and the stench of liquor coming off him almost made her gag. She touched the back of his head gingerly and her fingers came away crimson.

'Mr Shonto! Please stand up!'

She couldn't lift him, but approaching at that moment from behind was someone much stronger and seemingly impervious to the elements.

'Polly Gearin!' said Miss Henson. 'Would you be good enough to apprise me of what any young lady might be doing out in a public street in her night attire in the small hours in the company of an obvious drunken inebriate?'

'Oh, Miss Henson,' Polly cried, straightening. 'He's not drunk. He's injured. I suspect he must have fallen somewhere. Please help me get him inside before this storm really hits.'

Miss Henson planted work-reddened fists upon angular hips and shook her head. She weighed but ninety-seven pounds in her chemise and Polly didn't weigh much more. Assessing the kneeling figure, she again shook her head. No way could they shift that sodden weight, she considered. And even if they could she would not permit an adult male inside her establishment at this time of night even in exchange for free tickets through the pearly gates.

She said as much, yet the usually compliant Polly objected. 'We just can't leave him out here like this, Miss Henson. Not in his state, we can't.'

The woman sniffed. 'He would appear to be in considerably better condition than those fellows he consigned to the hospital and the funeral parlour, my girl.'

The rain was growing heavier and Polly's robe was beginning to cling to her body. Miss Henson's spectacles had fogged up. Raindrops spattered down on Shonto's slumped form.

'Please, Miss Henson . . . '

The spinster pursed thin lips, ready to refuse again. Then a familiar voice reached them through the grey sheets of rain. 'Polly? What on earth is going on?'

Polly turned and ran to the young man emerging from the gloom. Billy Pickard was her would-be-suitor whom she barely condescended to tolerate from time to time socially. He was so harmless that even Miss Henson almost approved of him. Almost.

Polly was explaining the situation when Shonto suddenly raised his head and spoke for the first time.

'Begging for death! The world's filled with sons of bitches just begging for death!'

Miss Henson was shocked even though it seemed obvious the man didn't know what he was saying.

'The foul of mouth shall not inherit the earth!' she admonished. 'And nor shall the murderous, the profane nor the frequenter of places of ill repute enter my home under any circumstances . . . ' She broke off with an exclamation when Billy Pickard knelt and slipped an arm around Shonto's shoulders and was assisting him to rise. 'Young man, what are you doing?'

'Toting him inside, Miss Henson,' she was told. 'He could catch his death if we leave him out here. Give me a hand, Polly, the man weighs a ton.'

Miss Henson registered stern disapproval, but before she could protest further a slurred voice spoke over her.

'Begging for death . . . so they are!' Shonto repeated. 'All my life that breed has plagued me. They might as well go round with big placards slung around their necks that say 'Kill me!' They convince themselves they're fast and tough, but they're just fools who crave to die young. But, but . . . they can kill you . . . that's if you don't get in first . . . '

He broke off to gaze from Billy to Polly, but could not focus.

'I always get in first,' he boasted bitterly. 'Yessir, old Get-'em-first Shonto, that's me. Hell, I've got enough men first to fill a graveyard. How many did I get first today, does anybody know?'

He was plainly in bad shape, so they ignored his ramblings and hauled him off to the rooming house as the rain began sheeting down in earnest. Miss Henson almost slipped in the mud several times in her attempts to draw ahead of the trio and eventually succeeded in being first to gain the shelter of the porch overhang. She fought to catch her breath then stood four-square before the closed door with arms folded firmly.

'Not in my rooming house!' she proclaimed.

'Oh, please, Miss Henson,' Polly begged.

'Well, not half-naked, leastways,' the woman compromised. 'Mr Shonto, if I am to be forced to offer you the hospitality of my residence then the very least you can do is button up your shirt and tuck it in.'

For a long moment it seemed he would rebel, the scowl he bent on the woman mean enough to peel paint. But

62

in that short space of time the bitterness that had followed in the wake of the gunplay abruptly deserted him, leaving him feeling spent and very cold. He shook his arms free of supporting hands and obediently buttoned up his sodden shirt, finally tucked it in. Later, he couldn't remember the last time he'd ever obeyed any instruction when ordered to do so.

★ ★ ★

The singing stopped.

The preacher removed his black hat, emptied rain water from the brim then replaced it on his balding dome before launching into his graveside eulogy.

'Some might say that our dear departed brother, Felix Henry Baxter was a hardcase and lost soul from the wrong side of life's tracks. Others, even less charitably disposed, reckoned that the fate that has befallen him was nothing worse than he deserved. There are undoubtedly even some in our very own community who might go so far as to say that the hand that smote our brother down so swiftly did more good for this county than the rains that broke the drought . . . '

He paused to allow that to sink in before continuing. All around, the boots of honest citizens were sinking deeper into the sodden clay of Drum's desolate Boot Hill. Water shimmered atop the casket holding the remains of Henry Baxter.

For some reason, possibly simple curiosity seasoned with everyday ghoulishness, a large number of citizens had turned out for the burial ceremony. The violent nature of the deceased's demise had roused more than usual interest.

'And so, to the critical and the censorious,' the preacher droned, 'and likewise to the mean-spirited, the uncharitable, the casters of first stones and those blind to the essential goodness in every man — permit me to say one thing. Do not count me amongst your number. True, this poor fellow lying here before you did not always strictly adhere to God's commandments and at various times could have been justly accused of such sins as pride, envy, gluttony, drunkenness, lust, profligacy, greed, avarice, slander and failure to attend church on Sundays. But, my dear brothers and sisters, he was also a son of Jesus, and our brother. So, in retrospect and if the memory serves me right, he wasn't really all that bad.'

The preacher's memory was none too good. If the Feather River boys weren't genuinely bad, then all those honest citizens who had recently packed up and quit Drum because of their excesses in recent times had all scared too easy. Further, the notion that Bax had not been all that bad might have come as a shock to several former citizens lying at rest in this very graveyard, including the late Marshal Holder.

'He breathed the same air as ourselves!' boomed the preacher, warming to his subject. 'He drank the same water and dreamed the same dreams. We were his brothers and sisters and it ill behoves any of us to stand here in judgement upon him now he has left us.'

'It ill behoves us all to catch triple pneumonia standin' here in the rain all day,' a cowboy said in a stage whisper.

The remark was overheard, and somebody laughed. The preacher appeared offended, yet at last managed to cut his performance short on realizing the graveyard damp was creeping up his own black-stockinged shanks.

'One final goodbye to our brother whom we lay to rest here . . . and, I hope, this also means farewell to the Feather River boys.'

Women snuffled as their men lowered the casket into the red earth. The preacher possessed a keen understanding of just what was required at difficult times such as this. He understood that, to a Westerner, there was little more romantic than the demise of a fallen badman. They might well be feared and universally despised alive, but let them go down in a storm of hot lead and all the mourners then wanted to hear was how kind they'd been to their mothers, and about the time they'd saved somebody's dog from drowning in a ditch.

But the sparse tears were about all dried up by the time the mourners returned to town and set about the serious ritual of drinking and debating the events leading up to Drum's latest shoot-out in more thoughtful detail.

The Feather River boys would seem to be on their last legs after this.

This was both the general assumption and a cause for some celebration, for the battered Shacklock and wounded Flint were unlikely ever to be a force again.

But this, as citizens reminded one another soberly, still left the lethal Wild Johnny Travis. And it would take a reckless man to wager he would be prepared to overlook what had transpired.

'Johnny sure ain't a forgivin' man,' remarked a storekeeper at the Panhandle bar.

'Ain't nothin' wrong with his memory neither as I recall,' a companion said. 'And that gunner's name ain't so hard to recall, is it? Shonto . . . '

'Shonto.'

The man who echoed the name was Mayor Collier, standing nearby with the lawyer and the saloon man. Sober and stern as befitted anybody just returned from a funeral, the mayor raked the crowded bar room with his sober gaze as though half expecting to see Shonto's lean frame materialize. But Shonto was no place to be seen. He had not been sighted since Red Hetty's bouncers had carted him away to sleep it off.

There was a rumour abroad that he was resting up at Miss Henson's Rooming House for Gentlewomen, but this was widely discounted by those who knew Rose Henson. A brawling, boozing gunfighter in her rooming house among her precious pot plants and refined young women? Not likely.

'Funny thing about that ruckus at Red Hetty's last night,' the lawyer murmured. 'That Shonto showing up drunk after the gunplay, I mean. I've heard those fast guns never drink to excess for fear someone might creep up behind them and get to blow them away. So, how come he was tanked?'

There was a silence while they considered this. Collier eventually sighed and cleared his throat.

'In any case,' he said soberly, 'what we must do right now is consider how this latest outbreak of violence may affect business and trade. Will it scare off more people than it will inevitably attract — people of the wrong kind, of course.'

The saloonkeeper and the lawyer exchanged a glance. Many believed Collier had a cash register where his soul should be. He could always be relied upon to translate any event, good or bad, into dollar terms. Greed was both his strength and weakness. Although wealthy by Gila standards, Collier didn't have anything like enough of the world's riches. He wanted more.

Questioned once by one of his women on what he wanted most out of life, Collier had been momentarily nonplussed until he suddenly came up with the answer. 'More!' That was it. He wanted more business, cattle, shares, mining claims, partnerships, projects and big deals. More of everything. And there were times, when late at night with a bottle handy and his brain humming with big plans, he had the certain-sure feeling he would never be truly content until he had it all.

In the meantime they must view recent events only in terms of how it might affect themselves. Drum was already suffering from a consistent dwindling in population due solely to violence and general instability. Recent shootings would be bound to have repercussions. And if Shonto remained here, it seemed almost certain Wild

Johnny would show up sooner or later looking for revenge, which might signal even worse trouble to come.

At that point Collier said thoughtfully, 'If only we could attract a peace officer with the ability to stand up to the hellions. With a real lawman wearing a badge and enforcing the law — but not so strictly as to discourage commerce and new enterprises, mind you — Drum could have the best of both worlds.'

Heads nodded politely. But they were in no way convinced. They had heard all this before. Many times from many people. Collier's plea fell on deaf ears. They knew the man only wished to be free to go ahead with his crooked gambling games, shifty business deals and various shady ventures — but without the risk of getting shot to doll rags or having the town burned down around his ears.

Each successive peace officer Drum had hired thus far had failed for one reason or another.

71

But the mayor never gave up hoping, scheming and planning how things might still be turned around in his troubled town. Times like this he could get a little desperate, as the others well knew. Even so, they were genuinely shocked, when, following a long silence, he finally thumped the bench before him and actually named a possible replacement for the late Marshal Holder.

So hostile was the reaction from his audience that before the evening was out Collier was forced to shelve his suggestion.

But it would not be forgotten.

5

Dark Wind Comin'

For a cheerful young man with a naturally bright disposition, Billy Pickard could compose some remarkably gloomy verse, when in the mood. The four-liner he recited late next afternoon while gazing from the window of his rooming house parlor at the rain, for instance:

Dark wind comin'
Deep night will fall,
Desolation and disaster
Overtaking us all.

'Honestly, Billy Pickard!' Polly Gearin chided, wrapping fresh bandaging around Shonto's left hand which he'd skinned during his recent binge. 'Don't you have anything better to do than dream up rubbish that will only make folks feel worse?'

Billy smiled, a good-looking youth with yellow hair and innocent blue eyes.

'You never seem to understand, Polly. Poetry don't have to be cheerful or happy. It's supposed to reflect how you really feel.'

'So, is that how you feel right now, kid?' Shonto growled, brushing the girl aside and rising.

'Of course it isn't,' Polly defended. 'He doesn't have a pessimistic bone in his body.'

'Not pessimistic, just realistic,' Billy insisted soberly. He spread his hands. 'Men die like flies around here, and it's always getting worse. Soon it won't be safe for anybody on the streets but gunmen, and things could never get worse than that.' He paused a moment, glancing at Shonto. 'Nothing personal, you understand, Mr Shonto.'

Some insisted on calling him 'mister', and it made him feel old. Like now. Shonto reached for his hat but Polly beat him to it, scooping it up from the couch then holding it behind her back out of his reach.

'You surely can't be thinking of going anywhere, Mr Shonto?' she challenged.

'You bet I am.'

'You are not well enough.'

'I'm strong as a horse. The hat!'

'Best give it to him, Miss Polly.' Miss Henry sniffed with vast disapproval. 'It's my assumption that he simply can't wait to set off and level accounts with somebody — or anybody — whom he feels might warrant it, for whatever reason. I mean, have we forgotten Wild Johnny already?'

Shonto's face turned cold. The dead man had attempted to murder him, yet some appeared to want to regard him as a martyr.

'Is that what you have in mind, Mr Shonto?' Polly asked.

Shonto massaged his skull and grimaced. His drinking binge in the wake of the gunplay was anything but customary. In truth, he hadn't reacted that way in a long spell. Doing so had been dangerous, for he would certainly have been vulnerable had some enemy come after him with a gun. Yet he knew he'd had to drink to ease the way he'd felt in the aftermath of the shooting . . . and that surely was no way for any gunfighter to be acting. Was it?

'Much obliged,' he murmured, turning to go. He threw Miss Henson a half salute. 'And to you too, ma'am. You know, I've a feeling you're not half as vinegary as you act sometimes.'

'Vinegary?' he heard her echo as he went out. 'So much for appreciation of one's Chrisitian charity. I warned you, Polly Gearin, that kind of man is not worth . . . '

Shonto heard no more above the thud of his boot heels, loud upon the plankwalk.

The hangover was all but gone by this time, and he only occasionally still saw two trees where he knew there was but one. They'd wanted to summon a medic but he'd refused to wait. He

76

didn't respect doctors. Or most anyone else, for that matter . . .

Passers-by eyed him warily as, walking straight and square-shouldered again by this, he swung into Nations Street from the east end just as the lamplighter and his flat-bed water wagon showed up at the far end of the block. Two boys playing in an alley stopped and stared at him as he walked by, then began whispering excitedly. He turned into the cigar store to buy a fresh supply of smokes, and the shopkeeper spilled his change and acted jittery.

Shonto leaned against the counter as he lighted up.

'Er . . . ah, nice to see you up and about again, Mr Shonto.'

'I bet.'

'No, honest. Everybody thought you might've been bad hurt when you went missin'.'

'Do I look hurt?' he challenged.

'Well, no, but — '

'Then what are you babbling about?'

77

He could be rough like that when the mood was on him, yet realized he felt almost guilty as he quit the store, trailing smoke. Was that simply the after-effects of what had happened, further exacerbated by the booze? Or might it be something else?

'Like what?' he asked aloud but no ready answer came to mind.

The cigar clamped between his teeth was doing its healing work by the time he halted by a lamp post to survey the main stem. He was aware that this urge to drown everything out in whiskey in the wake of gunplay was growing more frequent. And whenever he attempted to list the names and numbers of men he'd faced down on one Western street or another, he was aware it was surely growing too long.

He straightened from the post and stared down-street at the livery stables. Wolf would be expecting him, wondering why he hadn't been along to feed him like he did most mornings. The horse would be rested and feeling ready for the trail, and maybe that wasn't a bad notion.

Plainly there was nothing more than further trouble for him here, and he certainly wasn't too proud or stiff-necked simply to ride away and have folks claim that he felt guilty over the death of Felix Baxter. Shonto never brooded on incidents like that. They could say whatever they pleased about him — just so long as they didn't try to interfere with his freedom.

He grinned sardonically. Was there such a thing as freedom for any man who, because of his rep and drifting way of life, could only lay claim to gun skills and very little else at twenty-seven years of age?

His smile turned genuine as he flicked away the butt. He still felt a little thick in the head and sluggish too — which was no way for any hard man to operate. 'Walk it off, pilgrim,' he muttered and set off to do just that as he headed down the central block, one thumb hooked in shell belt, and shirt still buttoned as instructed by Miss Henson.

His thoughts drifted to Polly Gearin. He'd all but forgotten girls were ever that young and trusting. It had taken real grit for her to venture out to take care of him; but for her he might still be lying in the mud of this hick town.

His smile faded when he caught his reflection in a window glass. Why was he hitting the bottle whenever he used the gun? Either it was a sign he was running out of courage, or something deeper. But deeper — like what?

'When in doubt, do nothing,' he advised himself and kept on until he encountered Mayor Collier, accompanied as always by bodyguards Mash and Poulter.

'Ah-hah, my dear fellow.' Collier was all smiles. His shirt was stiffly starched and immaculately white. Although attired well enough, his bodyguards looked shabby alongside the mayoral elegance as the man thrust out a hand.

'So good to see you looking hale and hearty.'

His hand went unclaimed.

'Sure, it's real good,' Shonto said sardonically. 'I shoot your town up and put you all on the edge of your chairs . . . and you're all tickled to see me up and about and ready to do more damage. The hell you are!'

It took more than that to erase the mayor's empty smile. Folding his arms and cocking his head to one side, he studied the gunfighter with keener interest.

'You had the courage to do what you must against the Feather River boys, Mr Shonto. You assumed rightly they'd come here after you over what happened to Shacklock, and your response was completely justifiable. It was you or them, and I could not be more pleased with the outcome. Had we had a peace officer here when they arrived, that might well have prevented bloodshed. But as we didn't, you were obliged to defend yourself and, in doing so, defended all of us. And I must add that I've never seen anyone defend himself better.'

Shonto scowled suspiciously, wondering what might be behind this soft soap.

'You want to borrow money, Collier? Is that it?'

The mayor chuckled.

'Ahh, you're a man of some wit as well, Shonto. You know, it's just too bad we shall be losing you in time.'

'How come?'

'Well, I just feel it would be regrettable should you elect to move on before you've had a proper chance to adjust to our town, and vice versa.'

'I guess I'd already seen all I needed to of your town the night I rode in and saw you hanging your marshal.'

'Saw *them* hanging him, Mr Shonto,' Collier was swift to correct. 'That breed of citizen who allowed themselves to drink to excess and go along with anything the Feather River scum dictate in no way represents the solid, strong core of Drum. No sir!'

'I still see it as a yellow town.'

'And of course you are entitled to your opinion, sir.'

Shonto gave up. It was like trying to fight a pillow. Your fist went in at one point and it just bulged out some place else. You couldn't really reach this breed. Collier, today, was plainly armed with righteousness and impervious to insults regarding his town. He wondered if the man might simply be yellow-scared of him, yet doubted it. There was something going on behind that smooth face mask.

He exhaled. Were he interested enough, he might have attempted to find out what lay behind that mask. Instead, he deliberately shouldered Drum's leading citizen aside and walked off without another word.

Collier called after him cheerily, 'You take good care now, Mr Shonto, hear? And be wary of dark corners and alleyways until things settle down some. All right?'

He was alluding to the Wild Johnny

threat, Shonto knew. That gunman's shadow seemed to lie across the whole town. He shrugged and for a long moment looked every inch the lethal man of the gun as he thought: should that gun-thrower come after him, he'd better succeed with his first shot. He wouldn't get a second should the first fail.

★ ★ ★

A pair of dozing horses stood hip-shot and head-hanging at the hitchrail of the Last Post Saloon.

Shonto halted and looked them over. Both were trail-stained mustangs, broad-chested, thin-legged and hard of hoof. Each carried a cowboy saddle with bedrolls and slickers buckled on behind. Drovers' mounts, he reckoned, and glanced curiously at the batwings. He wondered if there was a trail herd somewhere close, and if so, what it might be doing this far from the main stock routes.

'Well, hello there.'

He knew the voice and turned to meet the bold gaze of Red Hetty. She was smartly attired and carried the familiar leather satchel which accompanied her on her thrice-weekly visits to the bank.

Shonto nodded and studied her face for signs of fear or uncertainty. He failed to detect any. He was surprised by this yet heartened. If there was just one person with guts in Drum, even if it was a woman, then it prevented him painting the whole place as one hundred per cent yellow.

'Nice day,' he grunted.

'How do you feel?'

'OK. I reckon I drank too much and so somebody roughed me up some. But my maw used to lay into me harder than that for playing hookey.'

'I had my boys move you on at one time, so please remember they were acting under my orders. You were impossibly drunk and seemed to want to take my place apart.'

His response was a grin. He liked women who talked straight.

'Walk you to wherever it is you're going, Miss Hetty?'

She returned his smile. 'Most gallant offer I've had all day.'

They attracted plenty notice upon entering the bank. But Shonto immediately put everybody at ease by taking a chair and casually lighting up a stogie while Red Hetty transacted her business at the counter. Even so, the unlikely combination of flamboyant madam and gunman caused the tellers and security to have difficulty concentrating.

There were sighs of relief when the couple left, and everybody went to the windows to watch Shonto escorting the brassy madam all the way back to the bordello.

He declined the offer of coffee or something stronger and made his way back to the Last Post for a light beer and a little quiet time to reflect on his immediate future.

The saloon was able to supply the drink, but not the peace and quiet. A pair of visiting cowhands were tying one on, and their noisy wrangling with the bartender saw Shonto down his beer with the intention of trying some place else.

That was when the cowpuncher with the thatch of wild red hair reached across the bar and tweaked the bartender's nose. Immediately the bouncers moved in, but wisely propped in their tracks when the redhead, whose name was Bell, hauled his revolver and cocked it.

The bouncers backed up. Fast.

Shonto sighed as Bell and Faust, bolstered by booze and encouraged by the total lack of opposition, slipped into full hell-raising mode as they paced up and down delivering insults and threats.

It was just dumb hick behaviour, and yet for some reason it riled Shonto, seated alone with a half-empty glass in hand.

It took little time to figure why he was peeved. This was a yellow town which allowed a bunch of cowboys and hellions to walk all over them. He'd seen more than enough here to know that. Yet why this should rile him today was far less clear. But it did, and next thing he knew he was buying in and addressing the regulars.

'Goddamnit, when are you people going to start learning to stand up for yourselves?' he said in a voice that carried. 'What do you expect out of life if you let every loud-mouthed loser and stumble-bum push you around — or even let punks like the Feather River bunch walk all over you?'

For Shonto, that was a lengthy speech. His audience seemed to appreciate it, which he didn't expect. But the reaction of Shamus Bell was swift and hostile.

'And who's the big-mouth,' Bell challenged, rising from his bar stool.

Shonto sighed.

He didn't want trouble right now, wasn't looking for it. But that was generally the case with him. It seemed trouble gravitated to him naturally.

'Name's Shonto — ' he began. But that was enough. They'd heard of him and redheaded Bell looked both gleeful and menacing as he lowered his red head and charged in, swinging from the floor.

Shonto was fast and wouldn't still be around if he wasn't. So fast in fact that few amongst the crowd even saw the vicious right hook that smashed into the waddy's jaw, driving him back into the bar where he slid to the floor face-down, out to the world.

Shonto allowed his momentum to carry him within range of hairy-faced Faust who surrendered his own reputation as brawler and wild man in the split second it took to throw his hands protectively over his face and peer through his fingers at him in total panic.

Shonto lowered his fist, unclenched it. Somebody sniggered and Shonto turned his back on the cowering cowboy to face the drinkers who instinctively flinched back as he raised an admonishing finger.

He pointed in turn at each drinker as he spoke. 'You and you and you two . . . when are you going to learn to stand together and show a little gumption? So what if this town does have more of its fair share of scum and hardcases. Sure, this town is unlucky to have mean bunches camped on your borders like these losers. That's still no reason to fold up every time they feel like walking all over you. Go on bending in every breeze and sooner or later a big wind will come along and blow you all away!'

He moved across to the batwings, paused.

'Though I'm damned if I know why I'm taking the trouble to tell you something you won't heed anyhow.'

The batwings slowly flapped into stillness behind his back as he left. The drinkers stared at one another in silence, then at the still unconscious wild man on the floor. For a long moment nobody moved, then as though responding to an invisible signal, they breasted the bar and called for another round.

Standing at the window, Shonto saw, shook his head and made for Main Street. Why did a man bother? Then a bigger question posed: what was he still doing in this chicken-hearted town anyway?

While deep inside, for some reason he himself could not understand, he knew he wasn't ready to go.

★　★　★

Jack, Henry, Holly and Shacklock occupied adjacent beds in the little hospital ward attached to Doc Stedman's office and residence on South Street.

They were recovering — slowly.

Shacklock was still unable to handle solid food since having a poker table driven into his guts at great velocity, even though the doc said he would be fine. In time.

Henry's shoulder was heavily strapped

91

and he carried the arm in a sling. Yet he was at least able to get up and move around when he wanted, which was more than Shacklock could manage.

They hadn't talked much up until now, despite the fact that they were rated the gabby members of the Feather River gang. But the news from the Last Post saloon had just reached them and suddenly they were talking plenty — sour and bitter sounding, maybe — but at least talking.

'Seems that flash bastard must have got over his thumpin',' growled Shacklock.

Henry knew who he meant. 'Uh-huh,' he grunted. 'Must have a skull like a rock.'

'Could be the rest of him's the same.' Shacklock was massaging his midsection. It still ached from Shonto's body blows.

'Does anyone know anythin' more about who he is and where he comes from?'

'Does it matter?'

Henry scratched his stubbled jaw. 'Mebbe if we knew stuff like that we'd be in better shape to — '

'To what?' Shacklock broke in.

'Well, mebbe find his weak spot and then . . . '

His words faded and it seemed to his henchman that not only did Henry seem cowed by the whole incident that had seen them finish up here amongst the bed pans and laudanum, he seemed unable or unwilling to formulate a plan for revenge.

Shacklock had been formulating and discarding get-squares ever since they'd thrown him into this lousy cot.

He stared out the window, then turned as the other spoke.

'I reckon mebbe we was lucky that flash sonofa didn't finish us off when he had the chance — '

The conversation was interrupted by the arrival of the doctor and his nurse. Doc Stedman was the breed of whiskery old medico who demanded every patient take better care of himself, while he relentlessly abused his own system by chain-smoking and consuming vast amounts of gin. It was the doc's secret that he privately believed that if he had one chance of immortality, it lay in the 'treatment' of pickling himself so thoroughly with alcohol and nicotine that no germ or cancer would have anything to do with him.

Henry, Holly and Shacklock submitted meekly to their examinations. The hardcases' fires were obviously quenched, which Stedman was pleased to note. For over recent months, a large proportion of his medical cases had been gunshot wounds and broken bones resulting directly from the ever-increasing excesses of the Feather River gang.

'How long now, Doc?' Shacklock wanted to know.

'Well, I might like to hold you for longer, but I guess another two or three days should see you fit enough to leave,' the man replied. 'You too, Henry.'

The three traded looks. Somehow

they didn't feel as exuberant as they might have been. Seemed Feather River was going to feel half empty without Bax.

'Want a word of advice, boys?' the doctor asked.

They didn't, but they got it anyway. Stedman suggested strongly that when they were released they should forget all about returning to Feather River and go some place where they were not known and would no longer feel obliged to live up to their hellion reputations.

It showed just how far Shacklock, Holly and Henry had slipped when, after the doc had gone, they actually found themselves considering his simple solution.

But not for long. Help was on its way, and it arrived in the middle of the night when they were awakened by loud voices coming from in the surgery. Moments later, Wild Johnny walked in. Himself.

'Well, howdy-do, you broken-winded bindle-stiffs,' he grinned, brandishing a fifth of whiskey. 'So, what's been happenin', huh?'

It was a rhetorical question. Wild Johnny knew all that had transpired while he had been down south chasing guns and consoling a comely young woman whose wealthy older husband was off on a business trip to California.

As always Wild Johnny appeared relaxed, confident and brimfull of life — qualities rarely to be found in the profile of a killer. Only those who knew him well were aware that this persona which he often presented to the world could be a total sham. So it was that henchmen Shacklock and Henry suspected strongly that, behind his cheerful façade, the leader and top guntipper was spitting chips.

And they were right.

As the patients brought him up to date on recent events — up to and including their embarrassing set-to with someone named Shonto — Wild Johnny sprawled upon a vacant bed after scarily warning the night nurse that this ward was off-limits until he chose to leave.

Sipping whiskey straight from the bottle and swinging one leg over the side of the bed, Johnny was somewhere in his mid-twenties, tall and alley-cat lean.

He was, amongst other things, thief, rustler and road agent. But what he did best of all was use a gun. The speed of a hummingbird's flight was sluggish compared to Wild Johnny — or so a boozed up journalist had once declared in print. In reality, he could have made a fortune hiring his gun to powerful factions along the border but preferred the free and easy life with his pals from Feather River . . .

Johnny chuckled at some joke while inside his awareness that one pard had been killed and others shot up by the same man burned in him like a fever. Rare setbacks such as this were seen by him as a personal challenge, and it took willpower and a major effort for him to lie back and puff cigarettes, when all he wanted was to kill.

But eventually he silenced the pair with a gesture and flipped off the bed to land on his feet, light as a feather. He'd heard enough. More than enough, maybe. He'd been across the border on gun business when things turned sour here. He was ready to turn affairs around. Solid ready.

'So, where do I find him?' he asked, fingering back a curtain to peer out.

Shacklock and Henry traded looks. Of a sudden, they were feeling almost chipper and healthy again. Johnny's return was doing them far more good than old Doc Stedman and all his lousy potions and pills.

'Well, we hear he's been seen plenty at Red Hetty's, although they mightn't be the pals they were since the big dust-up.'

'We hear tell Shonto's got friendly with that Gearin gal and the old maid, Miss Henson,' Holly chipped in.

'Well, sounds like a grandstander like this shouldn't be that hard to find,' Johnny reasoned, eyes steely as he flexed his supple body. 'And if he's flashy, like you say, he shouldn't be easy to miss.'

The gunner's expression turned thoughtful as he fingered gunbutt with an almost tender touch, eyes turning distant now. 'Gaudy, cocky and hits the bottle — ' Suddenly he grinned as he made for the door. 'My favourite breed of prey. Bignotin' nothings just beggin' to die!'

Doc Stedman was irate when his patients emerged from the little ward fully dressed a short time later. Shacklock, Holly and Henry ignored his protestations as they hurried out. Both were still hurting some, yet they wouldn't miss the showdown between Shonto and Wild Johnny for a million.

6

Go or Stay

In his hotel room over Nations Street, Shonto considered the relative merits of staying or going.

Should he hightail, he reasoned, he could be long gone and likely halfway across the next territory before Wild Johnny Travis or anybody else even knew which direction he'd taken.

Where he headed didn't matter. One place was as good as another. Once he'd kicked the dust of this nothing town he'd no longer be at risk of maybe coming face to face with a whole bunch of hellions he didn't even know, all bent on bringing him down.

Times like this, Shonto the loner with a gun was increasingly inclined to take inventory of his past, his future — his whole damned life.

Of course, on the plus side there was plenty to be said for being faster than most with a Colt .45 as well as simply being free to drift just wherever you wanted. To be unafraid to stare anybody in the eye; be your own man; get them before they got you.

The philosophy of a fast gun.

It satisfied him, he reflected. Or had done. Maybe he resembled the reveller who'd stayed too long at the feast ... didn't quit when he'd had enough ...

Had enough?

The thought jolted him. He tugged the makings from his breast pocket as he moved to halt in the centre of the silent room directly below the drop light.

For a vivid slice of time he was seeing his past life as a whirling kaleidoscope of colour ... whirling faces, excitement, gunsmoke and danger ... and always the trail, that endless trail leading — where?

He shook his head clear and stared reality in the eye. He never stayed any place long, and that suited him. For wherever he went, sooner or later his reputation or his inability to simply stand back and watch everyday folks suffer would challenge one more time. Most often this eventually led to gunsmoke and goodbyes — then on to the next place just beyond the horizon.

Would it ever change? Could it?

He shook his head. He'd been down this road too often before. It led no place. The here and now was all that signified.

Focus, drifter!

His smoke had gone out. He stepped on the butt and began rolling another as he thought of the housemaid who'd brought him the hot news upon his return from exercizing Wolf in the broken hills north of town.

'He's here, Mr Shonto! Wild Johnny is back!'

He shook his head with smoke trickling from his lips. He knew who Wild Johnny was, yet had no interest in facing him nor however many other gunners this damned county might be able to throw up.

'Forget Drum and forget this crummy town,' counselled an inner voice. 'You let yourself get involved in something that didn't concern you here — so don't do it again. Forget the yellow citizens and what might happen to them if you quit. You'd be placing your life on the line for no good reason. Keep living like that and you'll end up in a pauper's grave and even those whose lives you saved will forget your name inside a year. Just ride . . . '

The whisper faded away and he sucked smoke deep into his lungs and failed to come up with even one logical reason why he should stay.

So he packed his warbag, slung it over one shoulder and made for the stables.

The liveryman watched in silence as he saddled up. Shonto glanced over his shoulder and realized the man was sweating heavily even though the night was cool.

'Relax, pilgrim,' he growled. 'There ain't going to be any gunplay tonight. You can stop sweating.'

'If you say so, Señor Shonto.'

'I surely do,' he answered. And hoped he was right.

Wolf made to bite him and Shonto elbowed him in the teeth. In response the animal tried to squash him against the wall of the stall with its shoulder. Out of patience now, Shonto seized one black ear and squeezed hard. Instantly the animal trembled and went still.

Shonto released his grip and was hefting his warbag when steps sounded outside.

The speed with which he spun clear of the animal and brought his swivel gun up to shooting level caused the liveryman to gasp and duck for cover. But both men relaxed when the slender form of Polly Gearin appeared framed in the doorway. Sensing another chance, Wolf slashed at Shonto's shoulder with yellow teeth. But he was already out of range, moving swiftly through the stall gate and clicking it shut behind him. Big teeth bit timber behind him but Shonto ignored the racket, halting before Polly. His manner was anything but welcoming. He didn't want company — maybe hers least of all, for some reason he wasn't sure of.

'Why so?' an inner voice whispered. It couldn't be the fear that she might have come to mean something to him. Could it?

'What are you doing here?' he growled. 'You shouldn't be on the streets at night.'

'I'm not a child, Mr Shonto.'

'What do you want?'

'I just came to say goodbye.'

'How in hell did you know I was quitting?'

'I stopped by to visit you at the hotel and they told me you'd left . . . with your belongings.'

His eyes narrowed supiciously. 'What did you want with me there?'

'I-I intended urging you to leave town. I'm pleased to see you didn't need any advice,' she added, nodding at the saddled horse. 'I feared you might be too stubborn or proud to act so sensibly.'

He eyed her narrowly, perplexed for a moment before understanding struck.

'Ah, I get it now. You figure I'm quitting on account of Travis?'

'Of course. He's coming after you. Everyone knew he would once he heard the news. But do please hasten, Mr Shonto, don't let me delay you.'

A shadow crossed Shonto's face as he studied her in silence. Watching from his doorway the liveryman realized how fragile and vulnerable the girl appeared in contrast with the gunfighter's whip-cord muscularity and stony expression.

Yet the gunfighter was uncertain behind the façade. Polly Gearin suddenly reminded him of all those other vulnerable folk who would be reacting to the report of Travis's rumoured coming.

'So,' he spoke at last, turning away. 'You've said goodbye, so hustle!'

Polly's face showed her hurt. 'I thought you might be pleased I'd come to say goodbye, Mr Shonto. I-I thought we were friends.'

It was as if she hadn't spoken as he swung up and rode from the stables without a backward glance.

Wolf danced eagerly in the dust upon realizing they were making for the wide open spaces. Stone-faced still, Shonto glanced back just the once as he left the last of the buildings behind. He didn't see her now, only the dark green crown of the cottonwood where the lawman had been hanged . . . the rear of the jailhouse where others had died . . . lights winking brightly from the upper floor of Red Hetty's. He turned back to the way ahead and once again was Shonto, the man nobody knew, receding into the night with his mind blanked to everything he was leaving behind.

Yet there was time for reflection once he'd dipped down into the long, low valley and all the old unanswered questions raised themselves again.

Such as why did all the old patterns of his life always repeat the way they did?

It was like a story told and retold.

He would ride into a strange town with every intention of maintaining a low profile. Play some poker to win, get a little boozed and maybe cosy up to some pretty woman, which he invariably did. Raise a little hell, have some fun if things went his way — then ride out.

How simple was that?

But things never quite turned out that way. People and places always affected him. He would encounter poverty, cruelty or some such harm, and before he was aware of it he was buying in and sooner or later gunpowder would burn and he would find himself again compelled to move on.

It had happened here. And should it happen in the next lousy town where he stopped over at, he swore he would quit drifting for keeps, hang up his gun and change the way he lived once and for all.

And he heard the wind in the trees overhead whisper, 'In your dreams, drifter. You always forget — the leopard can't change its spots . . . '

He swore and blanked his mind to all but the trail.

It would be a two-hour ride down the length of Eland Valley before he climbed to higher ground atop a gaunt, rock-littered plateau where he hipped around in the saddle for one final glance back. Only to see an ominous column of flame and smoke climbing the sky in the distance above the town he had just left.

★   ★   ★

Pretty Gina puckered prettily. 'I'm all tuckered out, Hetty. Can't I turn in?'

Red Hetty glided across the polished floor of her private parlour with a rustle of imported silk and peered into the adjacent room. Mayor Humphrey Collier was seated comfortably in a red plush chair with a glass of imported whiskey in a pudgy fist, smiling affably at the two cowboys while Doc Stedman examined their injuries. Instinct warned her that Collier had brought the hardcase pair to her place for a reason, but plainly not the kind of reason that usually attracted her male clientele.

She turned back to the room, drawing on a Turkish cigarette fitted into a fine ivory holder. She sighed gustily and gestured. 'Off you go,' she told Gina. She paused then waved at the others. 'All of you — get! I'll tend the bar.'

The girls smiled gratefully and made for the stairs.

The return of Wild Johnny Travis had thrown a scare into some tough young women not easily frightened. The whole town was edgy about the gunman and nobody wanted to be conspicuous or even anywhere within a mile range should Johnny and Shonto get to cross swords.

'Make sure you wake us up if anything happens, Hetty,' Libby called down, excited by it all despite herself.

'No, don't call us,' world-weary Carmelita disagreed. 'I've seen enough dead men in this crummy town without wanting to see any more of the same.'

They vanished into the hazy gloom at the top of the staircase leaving Red Hetty alone to return to the deserted bar room and her Turkish cigarettes.

She lighted up and turned her glossy head as Doc Stedman emerged from the dimly lighted parlour, his arrival heralded by a hacking cough, a windy wheeze then a shattering belch. As always, Doc's innards were a war zone of rioting malfunction.

'So, how the hell are they?' Hetty sounded weary and bored, and was both. Her interest in cowhands — either healthy or ill — had always been minimal.

'They'll live, Miss Hetty.'

Stedman placed his black bag upon the bar and took out his pipe, coughing like a one-lung consumptive as he lighted up. 'Heads like rocks and just about as smart is my diagnosis.'

He chuckled and wheezed. 'They still can't figure how Shonto whipped them so easy. I could have explained simply that it might just be on account he's fast as a wildcat and strong as a bull. But why bother?'

'You expect they'll want to make more trouble when they recover, Doc?'

'No chance. They might both be thick as planks but at least they're smart enough to recognize when they're out of their depths.' He paused to consider his own words, then added, 'I hope.'

The medico's voice trailed away and his expression turned uneasy as he glanced towards the windows. He sighed.

'I'm surely bushed, Miss Hetty, but a man would be a fool to try to grab some shut-eye just yet, I suspect. I'll most likely be needed again tonight . . . either me or the undertaker, or both.'

Hetty's face shadowed.

'And so it goes, eh, Doc? The first

man shoots the second man, and along comes the third man to get square before somebody gets him too. It never ends.'

'Some appetites and urges are eternal, Hetty,' he philosophized, hefting his satchel and grimacing when a twinge of pain struck from an unexpected quarter. 'That's why you and me will never be out of business. 'Night.'

' 'Night, Doc. God bless.'

Hetty sighed and reached for her glass. This town was surely going to hell in a handcart even faster than she'd expected. And if all the ominous signs were to be relied upon, there was even worse ahead.

★ ★ ★

Mayor Collier was quizzing his new acquaintances closely now, having caught the heady whiff of opportunity on the late night air.

'Two thousand head, you say?' Collier shook his head wonderingly. 'I never heard of a herd that size in this part of Arizona, much less seen one. And like I already told you boys, I'm the biggest stock dealer in a hundred miles.'

Bell and Faust grinned at him. Their hostility towards the town had all but disappeared by this. They'd ridden into Drum at the end of gruelling weeks on the trail with the cattle, were eager now for good times and maybe some business opportunities . . . who could say? But they'd run into trouble in the shape of a hard man with a gun, had taken some serious lumps but were now feeling more like their old selves again.

They couldn't figure the mayor's interest in them yet, but were smart enough to suspect that it had to do with their jobs as forward scouts for the big herd now bedded down some ten miles east.

'Sounds like you might have to talk to Sam, Mayor,' Bell suggested, tenderly massaging his head.

'Sam?'

'Sam Whiskey,' Faust supplied. 'Our boss man is about the canniest cattleman in New Mexico. It was Sam's notion to gather up all the cattle starvin' in the drought back in Chile County and set out on a drive until we struck good grass and water. He stuck to his guns even when some of the old hands were convinced he'd made a big mistake after weeks of eatin' dust and stock startin' to croak on us. But then the rains came, the grass shot up, and right now we are herdin' two thousand head of fat primes.'

'Two thousand head!' Collier couldn't help repeating the number and licking his fat lips. 'Are they for sale?'

'Sure as hell are,' Bell stated. 'Sam's plan was to drive 'em as far as he had to go to find a market. I reckon he's got either Prescott or Phoenix in mind — he figures only places that big could make a bid for a herd this size.'

Collier rose to pace the room. He had the whiff of a big deal involving big money, and his mind was racing ahead.

He was optimistic, yet cautious. He envisioned a big cattle drive coming to Drum with the riders drawing pay and spending up in the stores and saloons, especially his gambling layouts.

But obvious drawbacks loomed large.

This Sam Whiskey was travelling with a bunch of tough waddies who hadn't stopped over at a town in many a week. A yellow town without law and order could find itself in big trouble from a crew that size. Collier had been in Abilene one season at the height of the great Texas cattle drives to the Kansas railhead, and knew just what that could be like.

Liquor flowing like river water, a fight, retaliation, riot, gunplay — chaos. It was an old familiar pattern — and scary to boot.

Who needed to risk that?

Yet the image of all those fat profits just begging to fall into his lap quickly ambushed his simple horse sense. It didn't have to be chaotic, he reasoned. If you knew what trouble there might be, then surely you could take precautions to head it off. Such as hire town-tamers and restrict the booze flow. If a smart operator couldn't control a bunch of dumb cowpunchers and loser-town boozehounds, then he had no right being in the business.

Right?

Right.

The fat man was riding a fresh wave of enthusiasm as he slapped down several large bills to buy more booze when Red Hetty came rushing into the parlour plainly agitated and jittery, and drew him across to the main window.

Gazing out, the mayor of Drum saw a clanging fire wagon drawn by six galloping horses storming down Nations Street.

7

Wild Johnny's Ways

Leaping flames daubed Wild Johnny's lithe form in crimson and gold as he stood watching the jailhouse go up in smoke. Disgruntled to learn upon his arrival that the man he'd come to kill was no place to be found, the killer was convinced Shonto was hiding from him some place and this was his way of forcing him to show.

Maybe this was not totally logical but then logic had never been his long suit. He specialized in theft, corruption and gunplay, talents that had seen him grow rich and feared over time. He walked tall and was ever ready to assert his status, particularly in an instance like this when he'd had a close pard gunned down.

'More fuel!' he hollered to the

shadowy silhouettes upon the street. 'If this don't flush him out then the store goes next!'

If ever there was a time for citizens to unite and take a stand, it was now. For over two years Drum had been dominated by the wild men from Feather River, yet this was the first time a public building had ever been put to the torch.

Nations Street was packed with people further along, gaping in disbelief at what they were seeing and flinching every time a section of roof or wall came thundering down. They had the numbers to steamroll even a danger-man like Wild Johnny, yet nobody made a move.

'You bums over by the store better shift your fat asses!' Travis bawled. 'On account I'll be torchin' it next if you don't drag out that world-beater gun-fighter of yours from where he's hidin'!'

'He's gone!' someone yelled plain-tively, but Wild Johnny paid no heed. He'd ridden here fast to even accounts and might yet decide to burn down the whole stinking town that had failed to come to the aid of his brave boys when the shooting had started.

Those nearest the blazing store moved back from the intense heat. The red wagon, horses and half-dressed townsmen who comprised the fire brigade just stood and looked on as another wall came crashing down, sending cinders high into the night sky.

The last wall collapsed a short time later. The smoke and dust were still roiling across the width of the street when something moved in that grey cloud, something that took on a shape, a silhouette and eventually became the lean outline of a man moving towards a suddenly silent crowd.

Instantly alert, Wild Johnny backed up a step, right hand poised over gunbutt as the figure gradually took on shape and texture before him. Firelight sheened on a shotgun barrel and tinted the lean face a copper sheen.

'Shonto, by God!'

The cry came from the first person to identify him, Red Hetty with her hands to her breast.

Wild Johnny smiled.

The heat was at Shonto's back and his shadow stretched long before him upon the hot earth. He stood now with legs slightly spaced and his shotgun nestling in the crook of his right arm.

There was no need for introductions, each man guessing who the other had to be. Wild Johnny licked his lips and dropped right hand to gun handle. His eyes were hot and his lips were wet.

Watching the drama unfold from across the street by the livery stable, Shacklock and Flint stood poised and ready for anything. They were sure of the outcome, but should the impossible happen and the lightning-handed Johnny fall, they would be ready to chime in.

'You show him, Johnny boy!' Flint called in a breathy voice.

'Yeah, but better make him get shook of that there cannon first,' advised a tense Shacklock, his voice a hoarse whisper.

Wild Johnny was intending to do just that. 'No jumpin' the start, hot-shot,' he warned in a voice that carried. 'Drop that thing and we'll get down to it. I got a pard in Boot Hill that ain't goin' to rest peaceful until you're underground too — so drop it and let's — '

'If you aim to start shooting, go to it,' Shonto said in a voice of iron.

'Huh? What in hell do you take me for? Draw with you holdin' that? You think I'm loco?'

'This isn't a game, killer. I'm staging a citizen's arrest here and you're going to get your hands up and forget about thinking this is some kind of game. The games are over in this town. I thought I'd made that clear but I guess you are just too damned dumb to understand.'

A murmur swept through the crowd. Shonto had been offered the star but rejected it. What would Wild Johnny do?

He showed them with as fast a clean draw and clear as any had ever seen.

Shonto shot him through the right shoulder and the killer crashed to ground with a howl of agony. But Wild Johnny had guts. He was still attempting to haul his iron left-handed when Shonto loomed over him.

His hot gun muzzle rested against the wounded man's ashen face. Wild Johnny froze, while a breathless mob waited. But all Shonto did was kick the Colt out of Travis's hand then turned away.

The mob stood in shocked silence, listening to Wild Johnny weep.

★   ★   ★

Daybreak.

Shonto stood by the window barefooted as he lighted a Red Man cigar.

At last he understood why he'd sought refuge at Miss Henson's Rooming House for Gentlewomen the night before. Usually, violence and bloodshed made him crave things like women, liquor, loud voices, music and eventually oblivion.

But last night was different.

Following the gunplay, he'd told himself he was returning to this place to check on Polly, but realized in retrospect he'd really come seeking refuge.

But from what?

From everything out there! the inner voice chimed in. Refuge from congratulations, disapproval, fear. Whatever they had for him out there, he didn't want.

A quiet room with a gentle breeze stirring frilly lace curtains was enough.

He looked out at the sky trying to figure out what sort of a morning it would be. He recalled clear mornings in the past. Coffee scents in chill Montana mornings in wintertime, the fragrance of sage and summer mornings in the deserts far beyond the Gila River.

And far back there were mornings in the great city and a feral kid in coveralls who only had fists, muscle and courage to keep himself alive.

Later, there was total recall of a crisp, clear morning in San Antonio when a citizen named Quentin Farley came staggering like a drunk down the centre of a Texas street with his mouth stretched in a soundless scream and his face turned to the sky before he fell stiff and dead in the red dust, the first man to fall under young Shonto's gun. The day, the morning and the place that changed young Shonto's mornings forever.

A knock on the door.

'Come!'

Polly entered, crisp in starched gingham and carrying a delicately fluted cup brimming with strong black coffee.

'Good morning, Mr Shonto.'

'Yeah.'

'Coffee?'

'Set it some place.'

Polly placed the cup upon the washstand and straightened. She studied his naked upper body and saw the muscles and the scars. So many scars. She saw how gracefully he moved as he reached for the cup and how even when relaxed he carried himself very straight, almost like a soldier. He was at the one time a mystery, a symbol of violence, plus some third element which she could not as yet identify.

'Did you sleep well, Mr Shonto?'

'When are you going to stop calling me that?'

'But it's your name.'

'The name is Shonto. Period.' He struck a match and set a Red Man alight, smoke tatters rising in the still air. 'I was born Jack Shonto, *compre*? But Jack was my father's name and my father was a son of a bitch. So the day I got shook of him I dropped that handle. You get that?'

He knew he was terse, didn't want to be. He expected her to flounce out, but instead she stayed.

'You must be feeling better to be so crabby.'

'Crabby? I've never been called that.'

Polly's head turned sharply at the sound of steps outside. She appeared suddenly alarmed. 'Oh, please put your shirt on Mr Shonto. Miss Henson — '

126

'Can go and get — '

He broke off as the spinster appeared in the doorway, spectacles shimmering with disapproval as she took in the scene.

'Sir, do you believe the Maker would have made our bodies so ugly to the eye had he intended, in His great scheme of things, that we should go stark naked before the world?'

'Ugly?' Shonto grinned mockingly. He was suddenly enjoying this. This whole scene was such a contrast to the brutal reality of what had transpired overnight — an unexpected breathing space. 'Are you telling me I'm built ugly?'

Miss Henson shuddered with distaste. 'Ugh! Do make some concession to civilization and please put on a shirt, sir.'

Shonto deliberately advanced towards the little woman, dragging a shirt off the bed post as he passed. He seemed to be attempting to draw it on, but all he was doing was flexing his muscles, and the

closer he drew the taller and more threatening he seemed to become in Miss
Henson's horrified eyes.

'Ohh!'

It was too much for Miss Henson
who promptly turned and fled the
room. And perhaps for the first time
since riding into this town Shonto
actually smiled as he turned back to the
girl. He winked and she stifled a giggle
with her hand.

'You really shouldn't do things like
that, Shonto.'

He drew on the shirt and cast about
for his boots. 'Yeah, you could be right,'
he said. 'I guess I make a habit of doing
things I shouldn't. Ahh, there they are.'

She watched him sit on the edge of
the bed to draw on the boots. She'd
never encountered a man like this who
could chill and attract at the same time,
a man who appeared both cruel and
gentle, insensitive yet understanding.
He was an enigma and a mystery, and
yet when she'd learned he'd survived
the gunfight, Polly had wept with relief.

'If you're referring to last night,' she said, moving to the window, 'then you know you had to do it. There was no other choice. Wild Johnny came to town to kill you. Everybody knows that.'

'You know, every time I gun somebody down, it seems there's a real good reason for it, girl. But I wonder just how far that will take me when I face my Maker. I can just hear myself: 'Sure, God, I've wasted a lot of men, yet every one of them had it coming.' Somehow, I'm not sure just how much good that might do me.'

Polly watched him buckle on his gunrig. She rubbed her bare arms as though cold with her eyes fixed on the six-gun in the swivel rig. Firearms terrified her, even if they were as common as flies along the Gila. She associated them with bad men, but also with the strong. She supposed a man must be strong simply to survive. She had seen many men die by the gun, most of them young.

'Does that mean you believe in God?' she asked.

'Maybe I believe in a few things that might surprise you.' Strangely, he wanted to talk. Doing so deferred whatever might be waiting for him beyond this quiet room.

She smiled. 'Do you deliberately try to be mysterious and contradictory?'

He glanced at her sharply as he buckled on his gun belt. 'What do you mean? I don't see myself as mysterious.'

'Well, I do. For instance, why did you return after you'd already left town? That seemed mysterious to me, still does.'

He glanced away. 'Maybe I forgot something . . . '

'You came back for one of two reasons. Either you simply wanted a fight, or else you were afraid of what Johnny might do to the town if he found you gone. It was the same when the other boys came in. You could have avoided a showdown, but you didn't. That's what I find mysterious. I guess most everybody here does too.'

He grimaced as he fingered back his thick hair then reached for his hat. 'Maybe — ' he began, then cocked his head sharply at the sound of voices. Peering out, Polly was astonished to see Billy Pickard and Red Hetty climbing the rooming-house steps side by side. Billy was a regular visitor, but she had never sighted Red Hetty down this end of the street before, much less at Miss Henson's.

She hurried off for the parlour with Shonto following more slowly. Billy glanced round at them a little nervously before speaking.

'I, er, met up with Miss Hetty on my way here, Polly,' he explained. 'She was looking for Shonto and I told her he was here.'

'Looking for me, Hetty?' Shonto said with a grin. 'Don't tell me business is so bad you've taken up hunting for customers?'

Polly and Billy both reddened, and even the formidable Red Hetty

131

appeared uncomfortable.

'Nobody sighted you after the gun-fight,' she said stiffly. 'I was concerned for you.' She nodded to Polly. 'Forgive my intrusion, dear, but I thought he might have been hurt, and nobody had realized it.'

'Others may forgive you, madam, but I certainly never shall,' an imperious voice spoke from the doorway. 'How dare you!'

It was Miss Henson, quivering with outrage but anything but speechless as she swept into the parlour to confront the enemy at close quarters.

'What is the meaning of this, madam?'

Hetty looked her up and down. 'You don't imagine I'd be caught in a dump like this without good reason, do you — madam?'

'A dump? You of all people dare say that, coming as you do from a . . . a — ' Miss Henson couldn't bring herself to give Red Hetty's establishment a name. She flung a quivering hand at the doors. 'Would you kindly leave my house this instant? And you too, sir. I should have realized from the beginning that extending you charity would end like this. I should have foreseen that a gunman would only attract more of his own reprehensible kind.'

'I'm sure Miss Hetty only came here out of concern for Shonto, Miss Henson,' Polly defended.

'Would anyone like to hear my latest poem?' offered Billy Pickard, hoping to defuse the situation.

He was ignored.

'Reckon I appreciate you worrying about me, Miss Hetty,' Shonto said with a sly look. 'Just like I appreciate you letting me stay overnight, Miss Henson. You're both warm-hearted ladies, and I reckon you've got more in common than you think.'

Neither woman took that as a compliment, and Shonto winked at Polly as Hetty and Miss Henson started in wrangling again.

Polly dared not smile, even if Shonto

were amused. Leaving them to it, he threw an arm around Billy's shoulders and walked him out onto the balcony, his attitude towards these people entirely different from that which he presented to most everybody else in town.

With this dreamy boy, Polly and Miss Henson, he felt he could let down some of his defences. In this case, he also had a word of advice.

'That's an important lesson for you to remember should ever you and Polly get around to tying the knot, kid. Always keep the womenfolks wrangling, because while they are at it they're leaving you alone to enjoy life. Catch on?'

'Shucks, Mr Shonto, I don't know if Polly and me will ever get that far.'

For some reason he didn't understand, Shonto felt almost pleased to hear that. He frowned and said; 'Why not? You like her, don't you?'

'Hell, yes. But there's more to gettin' wed than that.' He shrugged. 'In any case, we're both too young.'

'Any man who writes poetry like you do is old enough for most anything.' Shonto sobered as he gazed along South Street towards Nations. 'Town seems mighty quiet this morning . . . '

'It is. They say Doc Stedman is considerin' amputatin' Wild Johnny's gun arm, so I guess we can say for sure that the Feather River bunch is all washed up now.'

'What about those herders, Faust and Bell?'

'I saw them drinkin' coffee with the mayor a spell back. They looked pretty low and quiet. I don't see that we'll be havin' much trouble from them neither.'

'If not them, then likely somebody else,' Shonto said soberly. 'That's on account I attract trouble, like it or not.'

'Gosh, what you've done in Drum is what most folks would have liked to do long ago, Mr Shonto.'

Shonto was thoughtful. 'Nice of you to say so, kid . . . ' He gazed around. 'In any case, now Feather River's out of circulation, Drum might get to stand up for itself.'

It was at that moment that Red Hetty emerged from the building, looking smug. She was followed by Miss Henson, appearing even more enraged than before.

'How dare you?' the woman sputtered. 'How dare you offer me . . . employment? Me!'

Shonto called to Hetty, 'You didn't do that, did you?'

Hetty was unrepentant. 'Why not? She had the gall to invite me to the next meeting of the Church Ladies' Association in the hope I might 'change my ways' as she put it. So I offered her a job in case she might like to change hers.'

Shonto reckoned that was the right time to leave.

He felt almost relaxed walking the plankboards beneath the heavy cottonwoods of South Street with Hetty at his side. A woman sweeping her porch halted to watch them pass by, then came down to her gate to peer after them, scowling hard.

'I can read minds,' Shonto said. 'She's thinking, 'The Gunman and the Madam!' Or maybe, 'The Devil and his Strumpet'. That's got a kind of ring to it, don't you reckon?'

Hetty studied him soberly. 'You seem to be in an easy-going mood today. I expected after what happened you'd be just the opposite.'

'We're an unpredictable breed,' he said, half seriously, half ironically. Yet he appeared to sober when he tilted his head back to watch the play of sunlight on the cottonwoods overhead. He shrugged. 'Unpredictable even to ourselves at times . . . '

'I was so worried about you.'

Shonto fell silent until he halted at the Nations Street corner to stare directly ahead. In both the woman's words and in her tone, he sensed a reaching out. The right response from him at that moment could bring them close, he sensed. But he didn't come to provide it.

'Forget it, Hetty.'

'What do you mean?'

He studied her, his gaze dark and deep. 'You know what I mean. There's nothing ahead for us, and it's day-dreaming to think there ever could be. Once, maybe, but not now. It's way too late.'

Her face appeared to tighten a little, and she reached towards him uncertainly. But Shonto had already turned away to make his lithe-hipped way along the plankwalk, giving way to nobody.

He was headed for the Sunrise Hotel but didn't make it. He was halted outside the Panhandle Saloon by the mayor's flashy bodyguard, Mash, decked out as always in clawhammer coat and derby.

The mayor wanted to see him urgently, Shonto was told. His response was direct; the mayor could go straight to hell. Mash claimed he would miss out on a golden opportunity if he couldn't at least make time for just a few words with Collier.

'Golden?' Shonto growled. 'You mean gold like in money?'

'Big money, Shonto. Keerect.'

'Who do I have to kill?' He was being ironic.

'Why don't you ask the mayor? He's waiting at the Panhandle.'

Shonto surveyed the saloon windows and decided that maybe he could use a drink before riding out. And while doing that he reckoned he might as well find out what Humphrey wanted.

He did so grudgingly, and it proved to be a mistake. The secretary of the Drum City Council claimed he'd been authorized to seek him out and offer him the post of city marshal at two hundred dollars a month plus fine fees.

He was astonished that anyone would have the nerve to come up with something so patently phoney, and the man was lucky to escape without a mouthful of knuckles for his trouble.

Instead, Shonto settled for shoving him over a bar stool then walking straight out again, heading for the livery stables.

He'd finally had a gutful of this crummy town.

8

I am the Law!

Shonto was packing his warbag a short time later when the mayor appeared in the doorway. He continued with what he was doing without glancing up.

'Where's your bodyguards, fat man?' he growled. 'You'll likely need them after I boot you down the stairs.'

Collier entered the room, chuckling tolerantly. Shonto was surprised the man had the nerve to appear under the circumstances, and the moment the man began to speak, he turned and shouldered him aside to reach something on the bureau.

'I say, old man, there's no need to — '

'Get!' Shonto cut him off. 'You come up with some dumbass notion to try to make me look stupid and you expect me to sit and take it? You always struck me as dumb, but I didn't figure you to be fool enough to run a risk like that just to — '

'Mr Shonto, Mr Shonto, you have it all wrong. I'm deadly serious . . . the whole council is serious. We're in deep trouble and I'll be first to admit we're clutching at straws in approaching you. But at least do me the courtesy of considering our offer seriously, sir. With that mob on its way right now — '

'You still here?'

The mayor made to respond but the glitter in the other's eye overpowered him. He found himself barely able to mutter an apology and a windy sigh before turning slump-shouldered for the door. 'Sorry to impose on you. I won't bother you further.'

Shonto paused to scowl after the portly figure as he reached the doorway. He muttered a curse and thought that either the mayor was a natural actor or he really was serious. He hesitated a moment longer, then heard himself say,

'Damnit, maybe you are on the level. But for Pete's sake, think it through, man. You need a genuine lawman here or maybe a whole squad of them, not a gunshark or a — '

He didn't finish. Although regarded as a gunman most places he went, he had never accepted the tag.

'What we desperately need at this point of time, sir,' Collier said, recovering his composure, 'is simply someone with the ability to stand against the common enemy, namely the lawbreakers, roisterers, gunmen and outlaws who've virtually taken over our town and our lives in recent times, as you surely must be aware.'

The mayor raised his chin and waited for a response. None was forthcoming. So he cleared his throat drily and continued, 'I am totally convinced you are exactly that person, sir, otherwise I would not be offering you this position.'

The man was good, thought Shonto. He could make you believe he was sincere and honest even when every instinct warned he was just another small-town big shot bent on hatching up some play or scheme that would most likely feather his own nest.

Then an inner voice whispered, 'But what if he's on the level? What if his lousy council is genuinely desperate not to be left without a peace officer? How would he feel if he was to hit the next town only to hear that hell had exploded here upon the streets of Drum after he'd gone?

Fresh graves . . .

'Isn't there anything I can say to make you change your mind, Mr Shonto. We really are genuinely quite desperate, you know?'

Shonto still felt he should just keep shut. Finish packing. Ride.

Instead, he said, 'So much so that you'd offer the job to someone like me?' He smiled humourlessly. 'Man, that's what I call desperate.'

'Desperate circumstances can sometimes invoke desperate measures, young man.'

'I see a town in plenty trouble maybe, but desperate doesn't seem to fit it.'

The fat man sighed. 'Well, I wasn't going to go tell you everything for fear it might discourage you from accepting our offer, but — '

'Tell me what?' he heard himself say irritably, inhaled deeply to calm himself down then, 'Come on, and make it quick.'

Collier thrust pudgy fingers into the slash pockets of his waistcoat, took a deep breath to prepare himself, then rocked back on his heels and for the first time during the conversation, talked straight.

'There's a huge cattle herd in the vicinity, Mr Shonto. A man named Whiskey organized this drive in New Mexico, so I'm led believe. His plan is to trail drive all the way to Phoenix if necessary in search of a market, but the moment I heard of the herd I was struck by an alternative notion. As you would be aware by this, I'm the principal cattle dealer in these parts,

145

and I have contacts and contracts with all kinds of markets including the railroad and the army. As such, I'm seriously considering making an offer to buy up this entire herd.'

'So?'

'It would take time to raise the necessary finances, but I'm certain I can do that. This would entail grazing the herd out on the Kree Plains for some considerable time, and naturally the cowhands would be visiting Drum throughout that period.'

Collier paused to smile, man to man.

'There's roughly twenty herders in Whiskey's outfit — twenty thirsty, pleasure-starved and ready-to-rip wild boys who'll have hard cash in their pockets for the first time in months. Women, dice, cards, whiskey and the occasional rafter-rattling brawl, just to let off youthful steam. And of course the brawling and tomcatting could and would soon explode totally out of hand . . . unless Drum had someone capable of holding them in check, that is. Are you getting the drift now, Mr Shonto?'

'You must be loco.'

Collier's fat face fell. 'What on earth makes you say that? I just explained how — '

'You just told me how this town could well burn to the ground inside a week without the right kind of law. That's what you told me.'

'I'm fully aware of the risks, sir. And that is why I persuaded the council to hire you.'

Shonto fell silent. He was ready to reject the whole damn thing, yet let the moment pass. He might concede the notion of hiring a guntipper like himself to curb a mob of wild cowboys might have some merit, yet he still wasn't buying it. He'd been sizing the fat man up as he talked and still suspected duplicity of some kind that might result in his winding up dead should he be fool enough to swallow the bait.

He suspected the mayor might have been able to prevent the lynching of Marshal Holder. That maybe Holder

147

had run too tight a town and therefore interfered with Collier's profit-taking, so had had to go. He knew this was largely conjecture, yet it was enough to harden his original decision to go.

He said so, and the fat man countered with; 'Two hundred a week?'

Shonto was taken aback. But not sold. 'Go to hell!'

Collier's control snapped.

'Damnit, just what do you want, man? You've been risking your neck against the Feather River scum for nothing — could have been killed a dozen times. Yet now you reject a small fortune for doing the same damn thing. There's got to be something wrong with someone who thinks like that. Damnit to hell — what sort of a man are you anyway?'

Shonto span without another word, slung his warbag over one shoulder and walked out.

He was on the streets and on his way when something happened halfway between the Sunrise Hotel and the Quality Livery.

He'd accused the town of being yellow and worthless. Yet as he walked the street for the livery stables he found himself passing the burned out shell of the jailhouse. This caused him to pause before moving on, slower now and thoughtful, his way taking him by Doc Stedman's where Wild Johnny lay on his bed of pain.

Half a block further on he glanced down a cross street to glimpse the grassy lot where stark white wooden crosses studded Boot Hill, which was twice the size it should have been for a town the size of Drum.

He slowed to a stop envisioning this town with a mob of wild cow herders let loose upon its streets — pictured what might happen to good folks as well as bad.

And like it or not was forced to concede that Drum really did have its share of good people . . .

He never did make it to the livery stables and his ornery horse.

Instead he stopped by to visit with

Polly at Greasy Abe's. He was still there, toying with a meal he didn't want an hour later when the mayor and his bodyguards along with three fellow members of the Drum Town Council arrived. Sober, respectful and plainly desperate by now, they'd come to find out if maybe he'd had a change of heart.

Half an hour later an expressionless Shonto found himself at the shell of the jailhouse looking down at the badge fastened to his leather jacket lapel which somebody had unpinned from Steve Holder's shirt the day they cut him down from the hanging tree across the street from his own jailhouse.

★   ★   ★

Business was brisk at Red Hetty's again with the Whiskey herd spread out like a vast dark stain across the mighty river flats ever since the preceding Wednesday. By Friday, Humphrey Collier had organized his initial cash down payment to Sam Whiskey, a large chunk of which had that day been paid over to around twenty trail-crazy and town-starved cowboys.

This was Saturday night and with Levis bulging with cash, a seeming eternity of hard work and vast droving distances behind them, the cowboys hit the town in full force for the first time.

The house on Nations Street was well capable of handling a rush, and Red Hetty still found herself the free time to take her regular half-hour break in her private suite around nine o'clock.

Traditionally this was Hetty's time to sink her first double brandy of the evening and put her feet up while taking a break from all the smiling, dispute-settling and all the organizational necessities which every capable madam must handle with diplomacy and charm.

Rolling smooth liquor around her back teeth, Hetty, for a long and pleasant moment appeared lost in thought and far away. There was solid reason for her mood, for the madam believed that tonight she had been propositioned more often by more men half her age than any other night of her life.

She had done her diplomatic best to convince them that the term, 'the madam is not available' meant just that for some of the Whiskey herd's younger riders.

The brandy was excellent and it was relaxing and reassuring to hear the murmur of voices and chink of glassware drifting in from the main parlour. This was the sound of dollars, and Red Hetty was in this business strictly for the money. She told herself she didn't care how long the cowboys were in town, providing they behaved and there was no shooting.

She frowned as she reached for her Turkish cigarettes. She had been on Nations Street last night when Drum's new marshal arrested a cowboy for riding his horse up onto the plankwalk. The cowboy was big and mean and full of rotgut, but Shonto had disposed of him in mere moments. He had then ordered the waddy's own pards to tote him off to the cells above the courthouse, currently doubling as the law office.

Hetty had seen little of Shonto since he'd stunned the town by pinning on the star. She had been as surprised as anybody else, yet was also highly pleased to know he might be staying on. She rated the gunman as the first real man to stroll through her doors in far too long.

A sudden quiet in the parlour saw her set her glass aside and go off to investigate.

Sam Whiskey had finally shown up in person.

The rancher cum trail boss was a squat man with sweeping moustaches tipped with wax, a goatee beard. Years in the saddle had bowed his legs to a horse-collar shape and he gave the impression of being both tough and smart.

Whiskey had exercized strict control over his half-wild riders during the long drive. But this was a different situation. His agreement with Collier was that he would hold the herd out on the plains until the price was settled. Collier was paying him by the week while he negotiated sale of his stock. Sam Whiskey now felt able to relax after endless weeks on the drive, yet had not struck the worldly-wise Hetty as the kind of man who would normally seek relaxation in a bordello.

She was right about that.

Whiskey was here only to ensure his men weren't gypped, rolled or over-charged. Nothing else.

Hetty introduced herself but Whiskey didn't seem impressed. He had soon moved off through the rooms asking questions and taking stock of the place.

From a doorway a lean figure watched. Harbin was the sallow gun-packer who'd been signed on to protect Whiskey and his drovers on the big drive.

The gunman's appearance and chilling manner hadn't set well with Hetty from the get-go. Experienced with the opposite sex, she believed she could assess most males on sight. There were shy ones, roaring ones and the amiable and easy-going ones. But there were also those who would seem friendly as pie until they took on enough liquor to turn suddenly mean and even murderous.

Harbin didn't seem to fit any of those categories, yet Hetty sensed something sick in the man's pale blue eyes. She'd already heard the cowboys boasting of his gun record but that was hardly a virtue in her eyes.

'Anything I can do for you, Mr Whiskey?' she asked with a smile.

The cattle boss turned his head to look her up and down. 'You'd be the boss lady here, I take it?'

'That's correct. And I must say I'm pleased to see your men and my girls hitting it off together, aren't you?'

Whiskey stroked his moustaches as

he surveyed the plush room. He watched a cowboy descend the stairs with his arm around a girl's slender waist.

'I'm never against a man having a good time when he's earned it,' he stated. 'And I got nothing against a woman like yourself making an honest dollar by providing the necessities of life. What I don't want to see happen is for any of my boys to get took.'

'They won't get taken in my place, sir.'

'Well, I got a notion they're getting gypped elsewhere in this town.'

'That's not my concern. May I buy you a shot?'

Whiskey called across to the tall figure in the doorway. 'What do you say to a drink, Harbin?'

The gaunt-faced man with the sunken black eyes crossed to the couple, as graceful as a dancer.

Girls turned to eye him up and down and caught the whiff of something unsettling, just as Hetty had done.

Harbin's features were blank and watchful as he halted under the chandelier, slender hands resting on the beautifully tooled black leather gunrig slung around narrow hips.

'Guess I'll pass, Mr Whiskey. A man never knows what he might pick up in a place like this.'

Sam Whiskey smiled reassuringly at a suddenly offended Hetty. 'Harbin's a man with strong views on most things, ma'am.'

'You don't like women, Mr Harbin?' she challenged.

'I don't like paying for it,' he retorted. 'Never have and never will.'

'Hey, hey! Got set notions on near everything, he has,' Whiskey chuckled. 'But that's Harbin for you, ma'am. Near too stiff-necked and proud to live at times, or so some might say. But I guess when any man's as fast with an iron as him he can set his own rules, right?'

He seemed genial as he spoke but Hetty detected the underlying threat in his tone. He wanted her to know he held a tiger on the leash.

She resented this and was spirited enough not to try to hide it.

'I have to remind you men that it's a house rule that when things are busy we don't accommodate non-paying visitors,' she said stiffly. 'You don't look like a client to me, Mr Whiskey, and seeing as your hired help seems to feel uneasy here, I'll have to ask you both to leave and make room for paying customers.'

Whiskey plainly resented her abrupt change of manner, but managed a curt nod and turned, ready to leave.

But Harbin didn't move a muscle.

'I never was kicked out of no cheap whorehouse before,' he stated flatly.

'You seem intent on giving the impression you've never been in one before,' Hetty snapped tartly.

'Why, I been all over and done a lot of things, ma'am. But one thing I never done was take any sass from any whore-keeper.'

'All right, that'll do it, Harbin,' Whiskey said sharply as husky bouncers started their way, clutching billy clubs. 'We came here to head off trouble, not start it. Let's go.'

Harbin's luminous eyes drilled at Hetty, who despite her grit and gumption, felt a chill. The gunman smiled contemptuously then turned lazily to make for the exit with his smooth dancer's walk.

Sam Whiskey followed and the dangerous moment had passed.

'That there Harbin,' remarked a towner with a hint of nervousness. 'He sure enough sets high in the saddle, don't he.'

'Stands even taller than our new marshal, do you figure?' pondered another. 'What do you say, Miss Hetty?'

Hetty didn't respond as she turned to her curly-haired piano man nearby. She nodded, and as the music tinkled out, took herself onto her outside porch to stand directly beneath the softly shaded crimson ceiling light. For some reason the madam was feeling uneasy and suddenly wished Shonto would come strolling by on patrol.

But he didn't.

★ ★ ★

The cowboy held the entire Panhandle Saloon at bay with his six-gun as he drew the bowie knife from his belt left-handed. He was standing by the poker layout where he'd just dropped a large part of his trail-end payout. That was the reason he'd declared the game crooked and hauled his .45 when the bouncers began to converge.

They weren't converging now but rather stood warily well back amongst the percentage girls, drunks, local citizens, trail herders and staffers while trying to decide if the liquored-up loser mightn't just use that big hogleg if pushed.

'I never rode a hundred miles eatin' dust and blisterin' my behind just to have my wages stole off of me by no crooked cardsharps!' the waddy declared, drunken, red-faced and belligerent. The bowie blade winked in the lamplight. 'That's why I'm gonna make sure no honest cowboys get took at this table!'

Slicing the knife tip through the green baize, he ripped upwards. Several swift cuts left the entire table top in tatters. Impressed by the results he then went to work hacking at the woodwork, his right hand still loosely covering the crowd with his .45.

'Never did trust Arizona folks!' he yelled. 'Now I know how come. You're all a bunch of dirty crooks, is why!'

The bartender rolled his eyes at Mayor Collier who stood well back from the trouble, sipping a whiskey.

'Are we gonna let this bonehead tear up your whole place, Mr Collier?'

'What do you suggest, Jake?'

'Hell, we could rush him, couldn't we?'

'You have my permission to organize and lead a rush.'

His tone was ironic as the bartender

turned to look hopefully from face to face around him. But he had developed a leprous eye; nobody wanted to catch it now. He finally turned back to Collier again, only to see him grinning cynically. Drum had deteriorated to such an extent some found humour in their own cowardice.

Emboldened by this, the drunk with the knife started in hacking at the polished roulette wheel, his actions inspiring drunken trail pards to come out of the crowd and begin overturning tables and chairs. Their anger seemed justified. A lot of money had been gobbled up by the crooked tables and virtually every waddy who'd bucked the tiger here had lost.

'Let's take the dump apart proper!' yelled a burly rider, booting the piano which twanged in protest. 'Mebbe then we'll get a better shake here and at all the other cowboy traps in this stinkin' town afterwards.'

'I believe I'll move on, Collier,' said the man in the uniform of an army colonel. 'This looks as if it might well turn ugly.'

Collier put a restraining hand on the officer's arm. 'Please be patient. It won't continue much longer, believe you me.'

The colonel was anything but reassured. Down from Fort Lincoln to negotiate the purchase of a sizeable parcel of beef with Collier for the army, the man had been uneasy here without an armed escort even before the ruckus began. Collier had claimed his town was now under control, but drunken cowherders smashing up a plush saloon were not his idea of control.

The batwings bellied inwards and Shonto entered with a shotgun held in the crook of his arm, causing the crowd to part before him like the Red Sea giving way before Moses.

A herder in the crowd hollered a warning to a friend attempting to pull loose a section of the bar. The disgruntled cowboy, armed with bowie and six-gun, whirled to face the new challenge. He reached for his Colt with a curse only to find himself staring down the muzzle of the shotgun at a distance of mere feet.

Shonto smoothly reversed the weapon and slammed the butt against the side of the waddy's skull, dropping him like a stone.

He stepped over the body to meet the suddenly angry mob and dealt with them in a blurring handful of seconds that left three more down amongst the spittoons and sawdust — and suddenly nobody was interested in raising hell any longer.

'You men!' Shonto ordered the drinkers nearest. 'Tote these bums along to the courthouse cells. I'll be along presently to lay charges and lock them up.'

Without waiting for a response he span on his heel and strode out, leaving a sucked-out silence in his wake. The mayor was smiling like a big cat by the time the last of the troublemakers was toted out with arms and legs dangling, out to the world.

'Well, Colonel, is that control or isn't it?'

'That most certainly is control, Mayor Collier,' the colonel conceded. 'I must say, I believe I'm going to feel much more comfortable about doing a deal here after seeing all this.' He hefted his glass. 'To the conclusion of our business together . . . and to your new lawman, sir!'

The mayor was ready to drink to that.

9

One Shot from Hell

Shonto and Doc Stedman strolled along South Street with Shonto deliberately slowing his stride to match the medico's slow progress. Doc was weary, having just finished patching up several cowboys injured in the dust-up at the Panhandle. Back on Main the usual Saturday night was still raging, yet it was only moonlight, tree shadows and a welcome quiet here along South Street.

Stedman coughed harshly and clutched at his guts. No matter how pure the air, his abused lungs still reacted to exertion.

'You're sure some advertisement,' Shonto grunted.

'For what?'

'For your own profession, of course.

You're a doctor, yet you're the sickest man in town.'

'I'm a sight healthier than you are, Marshal.'

'How do you figure that?'

'You could die at any minute — that's why. But I know I've got six months left, maybe a tad more. So, who's the healthier?'

'You're talking about me getting shot, I take it?'

'What else? So, if you're dead by midnight and I live another six months, then who's smarter?'

'I'd still sooner my chances than yours.'

Their half-banter continued until Shonto halted outside Miss Henson's Rooming House for Gentlewomen. He glanced along the lamplit hallway for a pensive moment before moving on. Stedman studied him curiously.

'You're a strange mixture, Marshal. You know that?'

'How so?'

'Well, that speech you gave about

folks standing up for themselves and not relying on you for protection from the cowboys, for instance. It all fell on deaf ears, no doubt, and I was surprised you'd go to so much trouble. I imagined you'd be more inclined to advocate handling trouble with that.'

He indicated the sawn-off. Shonto just shrugged.

'I won't be around here forever. But their problems will unless they learn that law and order's not just one man with a gun. They let the Feather River bunch tramp all over them, and now they're willing to let Whiskey's drovers do the same. They'll have to learn to take a stand or sooner or later the whole town'll go under. It's that simple.'

'Or that complicated . . . depending on your point of view. But I doubt things will ever change here. You said it right just after you hit town. Drum is pure yellow!'

Stedman lighted his pipe and immediately paid the penalty. Shonto moved out of range of his violent coughing attack to torch a cigar into life. When the spasm was over the two continued on to turn the corner into the narrow street running parallel to Nations.

Two evenly spaced shots sounded, followed by a rolling drum of hoofbeats.

Cowboys letting off steam, Shonto figured. No real harm in that. Not yet.

'So, what do you hope to get out of your heroics, Shonto? Apart from money and maybe a cheap funeral, that is?'

'Why?'

'I reckon it's a reasonable question. I mean, a man like you turns up with no past to speak of and possibly no future. He gets tangled up in all kinds of bloody business when it's clear to anybody with one eye that he could avoid it all simply by throwing a leg across his horse and riding out. Now he pins on a badge just as two score of wild men hit town, taking over a job that cost the last lawman his life. I'll confess to knowing very little about the gunfighting trade but I would assume a man of your calibre could make much more money at far less risk elsewhere. Am I wrong about that?'

'You're right. The only thing you got wrong is me being a gunfighter. I'm good with a gun, but I'm no gun for hire. There's one hell of a difference.'

'I'd still like to understand what you get out of it?'

'If I ever find out, I'll let you know. Come on, shake a leg, man, I plan to get back to Nations Street before first light.'

'You are a difficult man, sir.'

'I know it. I also know I'm the breed you favour on account I help keep your profession busy.'

'Let's stick to discussing your profession . . . '

'Huh?'

'I met a man tonight . . . an unusual fellow named Harbin . . . '

Shonto pricked his ears. He'd heard plenty about Harbin before running into him upon the street. The gunman had made an impression, but not a favourable one. 'So?' he challenged.

'So . . . I'd be very wary of that individual if I were in your shoes.'

'I watch every man who might be fast.'

'I wouldn't know how fast or slow he is. What I strongly suspect, however, is that he might be deranged.'

'Why so?'

'Just instinct backed up by experience over the years. There's something about Harbin's eyes and the reptilian way he moves that makes me extremely uneasy.'

'Just how I feel about myself sometimes,' Shonto said, trying to make light of the topic. 'But, seriously, I suppose if the cowboys hired him to deal with me, you'd have to believe he must be dangerous.'

Stedman halted on the corner, breathing hard. 'One fast gun begets another fast gun.' He sighed, then forced a half smile. 'Well, good night, Mr Shonto. And do watch your back, will you? I might be critical of your profession and your techniques, but I'll confess I've felt safer since you arrived than I've done in years.' He nodded as he moved on. 'You see, I'm still concerned about my longevity even if I can see the end of it . . .'

Shonto watched him recede before moving on his way. He looked in at the hotel then moved on to the Last Post, arriving just in time to avert a threatening confrontation between drunken cowboys and a bunch of citizens from developing into something serious.

From the Last Post he continued on to the livery to saddle up Wolf and head out for the Whiskey herd.

He'd glimpsed the mob by daylight yet it looked much larger by night — a vast, dark stain on the face of the moonlit Kree plains, a sea of cattle drowsing under the watchful eyes of sleepy night herders on horseback.

The trouble he was checking on revolved around a youthful trail hand who'd witnessed the big ruckus at the

Panhandle. The boy had apparently gone back to the herd with the intention of inciting the riders to return with him to Drum to bust open the courthouse doors, free their pards and presumably deal with the lawman while they were at it.

He circled the sleeping herd and eventually was surprised to locate his hothead roped up to a cottonwood — on Sam Whiskey's orders!

'I'm not here to hooraw towns or start wars,' the sober cattle boss assured him, jerking a thumb in the direction of the trussed-up drunk. 'No matter what town folks might think.'

Shonto stood before a low-burning fire with hands on hips and hat thrust back off his brow. 'Glad to hear it,' he grunted. 'And, just for the record, I'm not wearing this badge just to see how many cowhands I can arrest either.'

'You thumped a few at the Panhandle.'

'With the hitting end of my scatter-gun, not the shooting end.'

'They call that buffaloing, don't they?'

'How'd you know that?'

'I bossed a long drive to Kansas a couple of years back. They had a town-tamer at Dodge when we got there, feller by the name of Bat Masterson. He was right expert at 'buffaloing' troublesome cowpokes with a six-gun butt.'

'I'm no town-tamer like Masterson.'

'Just what are you, Marshal Shonto? Nobody seems quite sure.'

Shonto turned to go. 'Just a man holding the trouble down. Like yourself, maybe. So, how long do you figure you'll be staying hereabouts?'

'Maybe another week.'

'That could seem a long time, the way things have been shaping.'

'Meanin'?'

Shonto jerked his chin towards the tree where the hell-raising cowboy was now snoring loudly, fast asleep and sagging against the ropes that held him.

'You acted smart here, Whiskey. I

hope you go on like that for the rest of the time your outfit's here. You and I are bound to tangle if you don't.'

'You sure talk big for just one man stacked up against twenty, mister.'

'I've been bucking the odds all my life. Maybe I'll be brought down one day. But if I were you I wouldn't bet on that happening here. *Buenos noches.*'

'Yeah, you too . . . Marshal.'

It had gone one o'clock by the time Shonto got back to town. Weariness was dragging at him now as he pushed Wolf along Nations Street. Apart from the saloons and Red Hetty's, the town had quietened considerably. There were drunks afoot and drunks on horseback as he closed in on the livery stables, but they weren't doing any harm.

He brewed coffee on the potbelly stove in the section of the courthouse he'd appropriated for his quarters. He splashed whiskey into a pannikin before toting it upstairs with him to inspect the prisoners.

He found them sleeping soundly. The

big night had been too much for them.

The stairs creaked under his weight as he returned to his office. He grunted as he lowered himself into a swingback chair and swung his boots up onto the desk.

A good cigar was all he needed — for the moment. He had one in his mouth and was ready to light up when he heard the shot.

* * *

Harbin winced when the alcohol swab touched his cheek. 'Goddamn, that smarts!'

'I warned you it would,' Doc Stedman grumped.

'I can take anything you can dish up. Keep going.'

Doc was ready to resume but his body wasn't. He had to turn his head and cough violently first. He had been asleep a full hour when the Whiskey herd's gunman had roused him by hammering on his door.

Harbin had sustained three deep scratches down the left side of his face, and one had barely missed the eye. Doc asked the cause of the injury but received no reply.

But Doc reckoned he could guess accurate.

'They claim a woman has no natural defences against a strong man,' he remarked drily as he returned to his work. 'But I've never been convinced that to be strictly the case — '

He broke off as Harbin's steel fingers clamped over his wrist. The gunman stared up into his face and the luminous eyes now had tiny red flames burning in their depths.

'I didn't come here to listen to your babble, you broken-winded old bastard! Just patch my face, tell me how goddamn much, and I'll be on my way.'

Doc Stedman often railed against Drum's lack of community courage, and yet he was victim of that same shortcoming himself. He was a man of integrity, morality and Christian charity — but no guts.

Eventually the gashes were cleansed and medicated. Yet Doc insisted they needed padding with cotton to guard against possible infection.

'Then goddamn do it and quit jawboning!' the patient snarled.

Stedman worked silently and efficiently. He was accustomed to being hauled out of bed to repair the results of violence, and had no doubt in his mind that violence of a definable kind was responsible for the gashes in Harbin's mean face.

He would wager hard money the man had been cut up by a woman's fingernails.

'How much longer?' the patient snapped.

'Just about through.'

The door swung open silently and Stedman turned to see Billy Pickard standing there. The boy's mouth was swollen and one eye was half-closed. Yet far more unusual was the fact that Billy appeared enraged and was clutching his father's old octagonal-barrelled hunting rifle tightly in both hands.

Harbin stiffened at sight of the weapon. His hand stole towards his holstered Colt. Doc shifted hastily to one side as Billy nodded eagerly.

'Go on, go for your iron. You might as well as I mean to kill you anyway!'

'Billy boy!' Doc gasped. 'What the hell is this about?'

'He raped Polly! I was walking her home from work when he jumped me and knocked me cold. He told Polly I'd asked him to see her home. But they didn't get home. He dragged her into the — '

Billy's words choked off and his trigger finger whitened. 'Draw your piece, you animal!'

Harbin's eyes were stretched wide as his shaking fingers reached as far as the butt of his holstered .45. Yet he dared go no further as he stared into the yawning muzzle of that gun.

'You're actin' loco, kid,' he breathed.

'You are crazy in the head. I never went near your girl.'

'She told me!'

'Now, now, son,' Doc cajoled, easing closer. 'Don't do nothing you'll be sorry for.'

Billy's eyes flicked to Stedman, and Harbin thought he saw his chance. His right arm blurred. The .45 filled his hand and came sweeping upwards at incredible speed. Instantly the old rifle bucked as a great gush of fire and smoke belched from the barrel. The heavy slug smashed into Harbin's brow and spattered the wall behind him with blood and brains. The body thudded to the floor and never moved again.

Billy and Doc stood frozen. For a long moment, the only movement in that room of death was the curl of gunsmoke drifting towards the window.

'I killed him!' Billy gasped.

'No arguing with that.'

10

The Guns of Drum

Harbin was dead!

Murdered!

Killed by some goddamned kid in Drum!

The word spread like wild fire through the Whiskey camp, bringing wild-eyed cowboys from their blankets and clawing for their guns as they yelled for more information. Who was it who killed their top gun? And how? What was that damn marshal doing? And, maybe most important of all — what does Sam say?

All their questions couldn't be answered at once. But it didn't take long for an enraged Sam Whiskey to reach a decision.

'We're goin' in,' he announced in an iron voice as he buckled on twin six-guns. 'And we're goin' to get justice. Some punk named Pickard accused Harbin of rapin' his woman then gunned him down in cold blood. Naturally, that wonder lawman was no place to be seen — '

'Them towner bastards have been out to bring us down from the day we bedded down the herd, Sam!' red-headed Shamus Bell accused. 'Fleecin' us left, right and centre, treatin' us like dirt and that Shonto trompin' all over us. I can tell you now, Harb's killers will get away with this latest thing unless we deal with it. Them yeller bastards was scared of Harb, and they set out deliberate to put him in the ground. They're all in it, that marshal just like the rest of 'em. I say they all gotta pay, down to the last man!'

The throaty roar of approval that greeted Bell's words brought sleepy-eyed cattle lumbering to their feet. Quickly, the nighthawks moved in to quieten them down. They succeeded, with the exception of Old Nick, the wall-eyed longhorn. He'd earned the name on the drive by giving more trouble than the rest of the mob put together — the biggest and the worst.

The animal began pawing and bellowing and throwing up dirt, riled at being roused. A herder jumped off his horse and threaded his way through the rapidly stirring cattle to broadcast fresh feed intended to pacify the beeves. By the time Old Nick had been encouraged to eat and quit acting up, Sam Whiskey was leading a squad of grim-faced waddies down the trail for the town.

'Consarn and damnation!' shouted the man delegated to stay behind. He hurled his hat to the ground, not caring if he startled the half-awake mob or not. This promised to be the most exciting night of the whole damned drive, yet he'd been left to play nursemaid!

The wall-eyed steer chomped on cut hay and watched the cowhand with a wicked eye. Product of a wilderness strain of longhorn, the beast was wide awake now and ready to raise hell, but the man retrieved his hat and waved a quirt in the critter's face. It tossed its head and then moved off with a snort to look for grass.

* * *

'Drink this,' Shonto ordered.

Billy shook his head. 'I can't. I never touch liquor.'

'You're going to need it,' Shonto insisted, forcing the glass into his hand. 'Get it down.'

Looking wretched and pale, Billy tipped some of the spirits into his mouth and swallowed. As he coughed and spluttered, Polly Gearin entered the parlour from her room. She had washed her face and brushed her hair, Shonto noted. True grit, he thought. Some had it and some didn't. It often took a crisis to separate the haves from the have-nots, and this was surely a crisis.

'I'm glad you came, Shonto,' she said calmly, drawing in a deep breath as she glanced across at the boy. 'But how did you know Billy was here?'

'Guessed,' Shonto grunted. His hand fell on Billy's shoulder. 'How do you feel now?'

'All right,' Billy said, getting up. He glanced from one to the other. 'Ready to face the medicine, I guess.'

'What medicine?' Shonto growled. 'Nobody's touching you, kid. There's no law against snapping off a rattle-snake's head, and that's all you did tonight. I'd have done the same thing if I'd reached Harbin first.'

'And so would I!'

Miss Henson seemed to appear from nowhere, fully dressed and toting a steaming coffee pot. There was colour in her cheeks and the hint of sparkle behind her pince nez. After years of rigid self-discipline she was responding to a challenge to her safety and that of others around her. 'An eye for an eye and a tooth for a tooth,' she declared. 'I never met that Harbin fellow, but I know he received exactly what he deserved.'

As the woman put her arm around Polly's shoulders and squeezed, Shonto swung away and strode out to investigate the rumble of distant hoofbeats.

Standing on the porch with his scatter gun Shonto picked up the racket of riders pouring into Nations Street. A six-gun roared, followed by hoarse shouting.

What had been bound to begin, had already begun.

It grew ominously quiet as Billy, Polly and Miss Henson joined Shonto to watch a vast cloud of yellow dust drifting over the rooftops, suggesting that the incoming horsemen had halted on the central block.

Soon the yelling began again, followed by the crash and tinkle of breaking glass. Then a voice, louder than the rest, rose in a shout; 'Come on out, Pickard! We got a rope for you, you little bastard!'

186

This was greeted by a deep-throated roar that chilled the listeners, with the exception of Shonto. He had lived through many situations much like this one as a result either of trouble seeking him out, or his going looking for it. He was never quite sure which, yet did know he never could or would turn his back on any town in a situation as uncertain as this.

'I'm going to bust up that bunch before it gets right out of hand. Billy, you stay here and don't show your goddamn face — hear?'

'Don't be a fool, sir,' chided Miss Henson. 'Just listen to those hellions. They'll tear you to pieces if you interfere with their villainy!'

Shonto hefted his shotgun, face set in stony lines. Of course he realized his life would be on the line. But it would have to be taken, never given.

'I wouldn't want to be the first man to try something,' he said, and started down the steps before Polly seized his arm, face white with alarm.

'Please don't,' she begged. 'They'll never listen to you. You can tell that simply by the sound of them — ?'

She broke off with a gasp as he pulled away and was off and running, a swift, lean figure with gunbelt, shotgun and lawman's star glinting in the moonlight.

Brief minutes later he gained a shadowed alcove on main street without meeting any challenge.

He lighted a cigar, and upon sighting the size of the mob half a block further along, realized he really did need it.

For there were twenty-odd riders crowding in front of the Sunrise, most still mounted and several afoot, kicking in doors, throwing rocks on roofs.

Directly across the street the funeral parlour stood ablaze with light as the solid figure of Sam Whiskey emerged flanked by three lean cowboys, causing Shonto's inner voice to make itself heard: *Don't you ever learn? How many times have you put your life on the line, bucked the odds and taken fool chances in nowhere towns just like this one? Yet you never learn, never change. What leads you to shoulder other people's troubles when all you are is a gambling drifter . . . not a lawman . . . never a real lawman . . . ?*

He had no answer. He never did at such times. He only knew he could not stand back no matter how many others well might . . .

A man shouted something and Shonto's attention focused upon him. Wild Johnny Travis had finally quit his sick bed and Shacklock and Flint now flanked him on the hotel porch. All three joined in the chanting which suddenly erupted again:

We'll swing Billy Pickard
   From a sour apple tree,
   Yes we will,
   Yes we will!

He curled a forefinger around the steel triggers of the shotgun and started foward. The mob was unaware of him at first, and there was another shimmering cascade of shattered glass spilling out over the plankwalks as somebody put a rock through the plate window of the general store.

'I want that bastard found!' Sam Whiskey bellowed from his high saddle. 'You hear me, boys? I want Harbin's killer and I want him tonight!'

He hauled a six-gun and pumped two deliberate shots through the Panhandle's windows. 'You treated us like dogs and now the boot's on the other foot. Give him up or you won't have any town left by daylight!'

The bellowed threat sent shivers through every citizen crouched behind locked doors or shuttered windows. The beast of violence had been loosed here tonight, and Drum's old weakness, cowardice, was rearing its head again.

Yet not everywhere.

It was only the ragged town drunk who raised a protest, yet it was a voice nonetheless: 'You men are all loco!' the sawed-off bum bawled from a darkened alleymouth. 'That mongrel Harbin attacked a fine young gal and only got what he deserved. Young Billy oughta get a medal, not a hang rope!'

A cowboy promptly rode him down. Another heeled his prad forward, ready to stomp him, but Whiskey's shout halted him.

'Get on with the hunt, damnit. If they don't bring him out, then go from door to door. Let 'em know that if we don't have him inside the hour we'll put the whole stinkin' town to the torch!'

'Hold up, you men!'

The sudden shout cut through the uproar with the force of a gunblast. As one man, the mob whirled about to see the lone figure standing half-shadowed upon the barber shop porch.

Suddenly the cowboys recognized him, and began to howl. But their voices were silenced when Shonto clapped hand to swivel gun and sent a bullet snarling between two ugly drunks standing bare inches apart.

The silence deepened; it was as if

Shonto's sudden unexpected appearance had caught every hellion off guard.

'You men are breaking an ordinance
against unlawful public assembly!' Shonto
roared. 'So, get your hands off those
guns and get to hell back to your herd.
And I mean now!'

It was an amazing sight — one man
challenging a mob. And yet such was
the impression he made standing there
alone against the odds, that for long
moments it seemed his bluff might
carry the day.

It might have done so had not
Whiskey suddenly cursed and heeled
his big horse forward.

'Murder was done here tonight,
Shonto. Cold-blooded murder of a
good man. We want Harbin's killer and
we got a right to him.' His voice swelled
to a bellowing roar. 'Who says we got
the right?'

Shonto's crashing shot slashed the
dust at the horse's front feet causing the
animal to prop and rear high, pawing
the air, stifling the mob's howling

before it could properly begin.

'The only right you've got, Whiskey, is the right to a bellyful of buckshot. You claim your man was murdered. I'm telling you he was stepped on like the snake he was. You sons of bitches don't represent any kind of justice and never will. You're just a mob — the ugliest thing on earth. So, be warned for the last time. Put up your weapons and clear off before I cut loose with this piece — and take it from me that's something you don't want to see!'

For hanging moments they gaped at a man whose presence and power seemed somehow to make him appear outsized and invincible to their eyes, even though he was but one against big odds. For maybe ten seconds, an eternity in that explosive atmosphere, it seemed the big bluff of one man against a score and more might come off.

It may well have done but for Wild Johnny Travis.

The gunman had been standing half-swallowed by deep tree shadows until he stepped forward into the glare of an overhead street lamp. Dramatic and unafraid, his appearance sent a shiver of excitement rippling through the mob as he coolly hooked thumbs in the shell belt holding his twin Colts and faced the common foe.

'You are in this stinkin' town's pocket, Shonto. They've been cheatin' and swindlin' these good boys somethin' murderous, and then you bobbed up out of nowhere to back them up in their evil. Even now, when good men are gettin' murdered, you're still stickin' up for their killers. Why, you are an even bigger phoney and yellow bastard than I had you figured — which is to say, a mucker!'

A storming roar of approval shook the street.

Shonto stood motionless for what seemed an age.

He didn't question his own gun skill or courage in those hanging moments, but rather was envisioning the hell that would result should the shooting start.

There were a hundred reasons for him to back down. Yet the final voice that reached him affirmed what he already knew. He must save this town or die trying.

And would.

A rider suddenly burst through the mob and he saw it was Sam Whiskey again astride his blood bay. Shonto triggered high twice and horse and rider slid to a dusty halt.

'Don't be a damn fool, Shonto . . .'

'I'll kill you if you keep coming!'

The big man's voice trailed off and again that lethal silence descended.

Until someone couldn't take it any more.

It was Wild Johnny Travis who drew and cut loose with his blurring .45 from less than thirty yards distant — the heller Shonto had once spared from death!

But the killer was now sick and one-handed, and missed his target. Shonto didn't miss. The weapon in his hands rocked the street end to end with its fierce bellow and the blast took the gunman dead centre.

Travis hit dirt and rolled with crimson pumping from a destroyed aorta as guns began to storm in response, in panic, in murderous moments of madness. In the space of a heartbeat the air was filled with screams and whistling lead and the stink of death.

Shonto dived headlong from his high position, struck the street with his shoulder, rolled and came up on one knee. Blasting from the ground and rolling defensively, he framed a target and squeezed trigger to smash Sam Whiskey from his saddle and into eternity even as his wild-eyed horse rushed out from beneath him.

The body crashed to the street to be instantly stamped into the dirt as terrified towners showed their real colours and erupted into headlong flight.

Swift as death, Shonto legged it across to the barber shop unscathed, from which defensive point he emptied his shotgun into the carnage before discarding the big gun and whipping out his Colt. Bobbing and weaving he fanned the hammer to bring both men and animals crashing to earth in a mad welter of blood as the sounds of chaos rose into an empty sky like the devil's chorus.

Nobody knew how long it lasted. It seemed an eternity but might have been but mere seconds. Yet the carnage was far from over and none realized it more clearly than Shonto, pinned down in the shop by the crossfire and aware he might stop the bullet that mattered most here at any moment.

Then came a sudden upsurge of gunfire from directly behind for the first time, and he whirled desperately to glimpse the improbable sight of Red Hetty blasting into the smoke-filled street from the shelter of the fire office. Moments later, heads bobbed up on either side of the madam and there were Billy Pickard, Miss Henson and

Polly all opening up with determination if not precision upon the enemy, causing them first to falter, then suddenly take flight.

Shonto quit shooting.

The Colt hanging by his side was empty now but it seemed it would no longer be needed as he watched the beaten and bloodied enemy retreating from the unexpected opponents — the finally brave and outraged citizens of Drum.

Moments later Red Hetty emerged from the doorway in back of him and he glimpsed other familiar faces behind her as the woman reached out and drew him through the doorway.

'You've taken enough risks,' she panted. Her face glowed with excitement as she gestured. 'See . . . the whole town is rebelling against them . . . you finally forced them to be men . . . who would ever have expected to see it?'

Not Shonto, for one. Yet he was proud that the man in the street had at long last dug deep, found his courage and vanquished the common enemy.

And the beef herders were all through. That was evident wherever you looked; dazed men, bleeding bodies, glazed visages and men on the ground, some never to rise. It was grotesque and yet inspiring. A mixed union of ruthless rich men and the greedy poor had sought the road to power and wealth here, but in the end had taken the wrong trail in the wrong company, and the common man had prevailed. Shonto was actually smiling grimly as he permitted himself to be led through the store, aware of the receding sounds of violence on the street.

Once clear of the store with Red Hetty leading the way, danger erupted again from an unexpected quarter. Two howling horsemen came pounding down the side street, shooting as they came until Shonto dropped low and blasted back.

He emptied two saddles with one fierce volley of fire just as a new danger erupted from an alleymouth fifty yards off to his right.

Two men, running his way and shooting.

The booming blast from the surgery window opposite sounded loud as a cannon, and when the cowboys dropped in their tracks old Doc Stedman revealed himself in his window clutching a smoking rifle in triumph.

Only then did Shonto believe they would make it — unaware that it was already over. For as the bloodied survivor of the two cowboys lay moaning in the dust and citizens peered out from doorways and windows in search of the enemy, a slow line of horsemen was visible climbing Black Hill south of town, making back for the herd.

The citizens who had at last and from some mysterious source of either pride or dignity finally found the guts to support the man with the badge, as they had failed to do so often in the past, emerged slowly from saloon, barn, feed shed, alley and alcove to stare proudly at one another, flushed with the victory over the Whiskey hellions and powerful in the realization that Drum would never rely on a single man with a star for their survival again.

It was a memorable moment for all, up to and including Shonto as, in that eerie silence that gripped the whole town now, he glanced over his shoulder to see Doc Stedman emerge clutching his rifle with a bloodied hand. As though this were a signal, doors were flung open and all along the smoky street more and more emerged until Shonto found himself surrounded by wondering, smiling citizens — and knew that at last he was free.

This town didn't need him any more.

★ ★ ★

It was three in the morning when the lean figure with warbag slung over one shoulder walked down Main with a purposeful stride.

He paused across the street from Miss

Henson's where lights still burned, was nodding as he moved on, surprised at the pang he was feeling yet not slowing to look back.

Within minutes he was in the saddle and leaving the town behind.

Wearing bandages applied by the girls from Miss Henson's and with a Red Man cigar clamped between his teeth, he was one mile south of town and climbing a rise on the south trail when it happened. Without making a conscious decision to do so, he hauled the horse to a halt and hipped around in the saddle to stare back, blinking like a man emerging from a trance.

What the hell was he doing?

All his life, he'd been leaving places behind, telling himself each time that maybe in the next town he would find that something that would bring him fulfilment and make him want to stay, only to find it elusive, place after place, time after time.

Until now.

Back there, he realized with a sudden

jolting clarity, were people who cared about him. They had proved it — Polly, Billy, Miss Henson, Hetty. He had come to believe that men couldn't change yet the men and women of Drum had changed that very night.

Something in his breast pocket pricked his skin. He took out the brass star and studied it. He was still entitled to wear it, knew full well there would be no rush of candidates to take his place should he keep riding.

He looked once more down upon the town. Surely a man could do worse than pull down a marshal's wage in a town that had found its pride — a place where he'd already and unexpectedly found peace at last . . . ?

The horse acted up when he was turned back — it was eager for the open trail. But Shonto's heels thudded firmly against horsehide and at last it broke into a reluctant lope, heading back to a town that had found its soul and the man who would help them keep it.

We do hope that you have enjoyed reading this large print book.

Did you know that all of our titles are available for purchase?

We publish a wide range of high quality large print books including:
Romances, Mysteries, Classics
General Fiction
Non Fiction and Westerns

Special interest titles available in large print are:
The Little Oxford Dictionary
Music Book, Song Book
Hymn Book, Service Book

Also available from us courtesy of Oxford University Press:
Young Readers' Dictionary
(large print edition)
Young Readers' Thesaurus
(large print edition)

For further information or a free brochure, please contact us at:
Ulverscroft Large Print Books Ltd.,
The Green, Bradgate Road, Anstey,
Leicester, LE7 7FU, England.
Tel: (00 44) **0116 236 4325**
Fax: (00 44) **0116 234 0205**

Other titles in the
Linford Western Library:

UNSIGNED AVENGER

John Davage

When Will Cord is shot dead for the brutal killing of Ali Toombs, Joe Hayes and his two sons know the real killer is still at large . . . Could it be Cole Sanderson — a newcomer to Consolation? Saloon girl Maggie Brown knows he's not who he says he is. Or could it be Lew Rosen, editor of the *Gazette*, who suspects the Hayes brothers? Fear and suspicion spread like a prairie fire — is anyone safe from accusation and violence?

FAITH AND A FAST GUN

Chap O'Keefe

Joshua Dillard, the ex-Pinkerton detective, on a sentimental journey to a mission graveyard in Texas, had ridden into trouble. Guns blazed around the headstones as he intervened to save a girl called Faith from the clutches of Lyte Grumman and his gunhawks. Grumman, a cattle baron, believed that a rigged poker game had lost him a thousand head of longhorns. Now he was intent on recouping his loss, whatever it took — and Joshua's Colt Peacemaker was hopelessly outnumbered . . .

GUNS OF PONDEROSA

Chuck Tyrell

When Nate Cahill and his gang take over the town of Ponderosa, sawmill magnate Fletcher Comstock sends for his friend Matt Stryker. However, Cahill is waiting for him. He gelds Stryker's fine Arabian stallion and beats him terribly. But Stryker will not give up. He pins on the marshal's badge, tames a rowdy town and gets rid of the ruthless Cahill gang. Now the guns of Ponderosa blaze and blood runs red in the Arizona high country.

DEATH RANGE

Elliot Long

Bullet-scarred Jack Cain, through with cleaning up gun-crazy ranges and wild cow towns, heads for Montana to buy a small spread and raise cows. But a hundred miles up country, he encounters nine-year-old Ethan Wilder whose ma is shot and near to dying. Will he come and take a look? Reluctantly he agrees, only to find himself ambushed in a hail of bullets — but what follows next turns out to be Jack Cain's greatest test — but can he survive it?

WILD MEDDOW

Caleb Rand

With a small herd of cattle and a big pack of trouble, Burt Lane rides into Northern Wyoming. Near the town of Clayburn, Wild Meddow is a neglected cattle ranch with no apparent owner, but Cole Dodgson and Vaughn Maber covet its water and fertile soil. Burt is forced to declare his real identity when Dodgson and Maber decide to overrun the ranch. Then a friend is taken hostage — and for Burt the time for long-awaited retribution has arrived.

VIVA GRINGO!

Steve Hayes

U.S. Marshal Ezra Macahan picks the wrong time to visit his cavalry soldier brother, Joshua, at Camp Furlong, New Mexico. That night Pancho Villa and his revolutionary forces raid the town of Columbus and though defeated, one of Villa's commander's 'Scar' Acosta, kidnaps Joshua's son, Daniel — and flees to a heavily guarded mountain hideout. But, as Ezra and Joshua pursue Daniel's captor, they ever rescue him when they face terrible adversities, a shocking revelation and violent death?